LONE STAR

LONE STAR

Barbara Barrie

Delacorte Press

Published by
Delacorte Press
Bantam Doubleday Dell Publishing Group, Inc.
666 Fifth Avenue
New York, New York 10103

Library of Congress Cataloging in Publication Data

Barrie, Barbara.
    Lone star / Barbara Barrie.
        p.   cm.
    Summary: Moving from Chicago to Corpus Christi, Texas, in
1944, a young Jewish girl copes with her parents' problems and
adopts a new lifestyle which alienates her Orthodox grandfather.
    ISBN 0-385-30156-1
    [1. Moving, Household—Fiction. 2. Family problems—Fiction.
3. Jews—United States—Fiction. 4. Corpus Christi (Tex.)—Fiction.]
I. Title.
PZ7.B275378Lo 1990
[Fic]—dc20   89-78075
                                                                CIP
                                                                 AC

Manufactured in the United States of America

September 1990

10   9   8   7   6   5   4   3   2   1

BVG

For Jay, Jane, and Aaron
and
Stan Margulies

Chapter 1

Jane Miller stared out the window beside her desk at the bright sky, where three small fighter planes roared out of the clouds, turned in a backward curve, then roared over the school and across the bay.

None of the other children looked up. They were used to constant noise overhead. It was 1944, and pilots were being trained at the naval air station. Jane's family had moved to Corpus Christi a month before, and she was still amazed at the planes and the brilliant flowers and the clouds shaped like giants' castles over the bay.

". . . up to the board!" Mr. Penn said. Jane jumped, but he was calling on Mary Cameron, who walked forward and began to write.

Mary wore a cotton dress like all the other girls. Jane's dress was heavy and hot.

"Mother, can't I wear something else today?" Jane

1

had said at breakfast. "I look like an old lady. Besides, down here the other mothers *make* dresses. Girls don't wear clothes from a store."

"Then you have the wrong mother. I don't sew." Mrs. Miller, tall and thin, tied the sash of her robe and took off her rimless glasses. "This dress is silk. We don't have money for new clothes. Besides, nice people don't wear cotton, and that's that."

Jane looked under the desk at her feet: brown oxfords. Everyone else wore sandals. Their bare toes brushed the floor. And she was the only girl with short hair. Everyone else had braids with rubber bands on the ends.

"Miss Miller!" Mr. Penn was saying. "Did you hear me?" He held up the chalk. Jane walked to the front of the room. "How many names can you add to the list of characters in *Julius Caesar*?" Mary had written: Caesar, Brutus, Cassius, Casca. "Surely you read this play in your Yankee school. You must be able to tell us all about it."

Yankee. Her face grew hot. Slowly she wrote Cicero, Marcus Antonio, and stopped. If she knew too much, she might never make friends here.

"Very good, Jane. Any more?"

"No."

"No, *sir,* please."

"No, *SIR.*"

"Did you happen to read this play in Chicago, before you came down here to 'slow Texas'?"

"No, Mr. Penn . . . well . . . not this version."

"What do you mean?"

"Well, this *Julius Caesar* is an abridged version for the fifth grade, and at my other school we read the real one."

"And do you think you understand what Mr. Shakespeare thought about politics and power and leadership?"

"Well, no, but—"

"No, *sir.*"

"No, *sir.*"

"Is it an interesting play?"

"Well, sir, it's not really my favorite play of Shakespeare's because it's . . ."

"It's *what*?"

"It's kind of boring."

"Boring?"

"Yes, sir. I mean, some of the other plays, especially the comedies, are a lot more fun."

"What plays of Shakespeare's would you, in all your wisdom, suggest for a fifth-grade class?"

"Um . . . *Two Gentlemen of Verona* or *Romeo and Juliet.*"

"Romeo and Juliet?" Mr. Penn waved his stick around.

"Yes, sir. I know it's a serious play and all, but the nurse is funny, and Mercutio and Tybalt have a great sword fight, and—"

"Did you read all these plays in the *fourth* grade, before you came here?"

"No, sir. My father reads them to us."

"Really!"

"Yes, sir," she said.

"You may sit down now, Jane."

She sank into her seat. Lowering her head, she carefully arranged the pencils and pens in the slot at the top of her desk. Everyone was silent.

From across the aisle Sally Garland glanced at Jane. A note peeked through Sally's fingers, and she whisked the note into Jane's hand.

"He's so mean. I'm sorry he picked on you like that." The handwriting was neat and round. Jane felt tears behind her eyes. This was the first time any of the girls had been nice to her. She took out a piece of notebook paper and wrote, "Thanks a lot. He really is awful and I don't know why." She folded the paper, and when the moment seemed safe, handed it back.

"Jane, what did you just pass across the aisle?"

"Nothing, Mr. Penn."

"Bring me the note, Sally."

Sally walked slowly to his desk. "It's nothing, Mr. Penn, really. I could just tear it up."

He held out his hand and Sally gave him the paper. He read it and stuffed it into the pocket of his jacket. "Jane, go to my office."

*   *   *

"Oh, you're the girl from Chicago," said the secretary in the office.

"Yes. Mr. Penn wants me to wait for him here."

"Fine." She leaned over the counter. "Would you like a glass of water? It's awfully hot today."

"Yes, thank you, that would be very nice."

"I'm Mrs. Wilcox. Here's some water from our little icebox. You just take it into his office. Whyever you're here couldn't be all that bad, now could it, hon?"

"No, I guess not . . ."

"No, *ma'am,* hon."

"Oh. No . . . *ma'am.* Sorry . . ."

On Mr. Penn's desk was a picture of a smiling blond woman with two children sitting on her lap. They all looked alike. If this was his family, she felt sorry for them.

An army of spiky cactus plants marched across the windowsill. Jane looked at the framed diplomas and the certificates and a large picture of a rearing horse, inscribed: ROPING CHAMPION, SOUTHWEST TEXAS RODEO, 1937.

How different Mr. Penn is from Miss Crawford, she thought. Stringbean-y Miss Crawford had been her second-grade teacher. It was Miss Crawford who had told Jane's parents, "Jane has a reading problem. Do you know that?"

"What do you mean? She reads perfectly well," Mrs. Miller had answered.

"Yes, she does, but surely you've noticed that she holds the book upside down?"

"It's hard to tell," said Jane's father, "because she sprawls all over the chair and reads with her legs over the back and her head hanging down."

"Yes, I think she's trying to find the right position or the right light. I know someone who can help her."

Miss Crawford brought Jane special books to read and gave her extra time when long division proved to be so difficult. Sweet Miss Crawford, with her little black mustache and her sour breath (Jane hated to admit this because she loved her, but it was true).

Mr. Penn entered and shut the door. "Sit down, Jane. Are you in the habit of drawing attention to yourself by talking back to the teacher and passing notes?" He sat in his leather chair.

"No, sir, I didn't mean to be rude. But you asked me about the plays. Didn't you want me to tell the truth?"

"I don't think a ten-year-old girl should tell the teacher which plays she prefers to the one that was assigned, do you?"

"But Mr. Penn, you asked me."

"And passing the note is inexcusable. You could be expelled."

Jane gripped her books and leaned forward. "Yes, sir, I'm sorry. I shouldn't have done that."

There was a pause as Mr. Penn opened a drawer. "But perhaps we'll just have a little paddling session here."

"Paddling session?"

"Yes, with this," said Mr. Penn as he put a long, heavy wooden paddle with two holes at one end on the desk. He took off his coat and stood up.

Jane stared at the paddle. "Are you going to hit me with that?"

"That is the general procedure here."

"My father won't let you!"

"In Texas we discipline students this way, and he doesn't have much to say about it."

"I won't let you use that on me."

He took a step toward her.

Jane darted behind the chair. "Call my father at his office and tell him what you're going to do. He'll come right down and he'll be very angry." She held on to the back of the chair, her hands wet and cold, her knees shaky.

Mr. Penn raised the paddle.

"Mr. Penn, *call my father!*" She backed toward the door. "If you hit me with that, I'll scream! The whole school will hear!"

The door opened. "Did you call, Mr. Penn?" Mrs. Wilcox glanced at Jane.

"No, I did not, Sylvia. Please leave us alone."

She slowly closed the door as Mr. Penn lowered the paddle. "All right, we'll call your father, and your mother too." Perspiration from his forehead flew in a shower as he turned and walked toward the phone. He swung around his chair and kept his back to Jane while he called. He put the paddle under the desk. "Take out your books and begin your homework, and don't speak a word until your parents get here."

"Yes, Mr. Penn."

Jane opened her notebook, turned to the section marked "Math." She didn't understand a single one of those little numbers, but she wrote busily. Her heart was pounding.

Mr. Penn took out a mirror and began to comb his hair. He straightened his damp shirt and flicked a handkerchief across the tops of his shoes.

In a while, there was a thump on the door. Mr. Miller, his shirt coming loose from his belt and his tie undone, stormed into the room.

"Now, what is this all about?" he shouted. Behind him was Jane's mother, fiddling with the brooch on her dress.

"How do you do, sir, I am Mr. Penn . . ."

Mr. Miller nodded to him and turned to Jane. "Honey, are you all right?" He tilted up her face and looked into her eyes. Mrs. Miller, her lips compressed, sat down and looked around the room.

"Yes, Daddy."

Mr. Penn told him what had happened and made it sound as if Jane had given a defiant, insulting speech.

"Daddy," she said, "Mr. Penn asked me which plays of Shakespeare I liked better than *Julius Caesar.* I just answered the question."

"But did you pass the note?" asked Mr. Miller.

"Yes. I've apologized already. Really, I'm very sorry."

"I know you are," replied Mr. Miller. "Well, Mr. Penn, it seems to me that this girl was responding to some fairly pointed behavior on your part. Did she do something else to upset you?"

"She seems to like to show off her knowledge and draw attention to herself."

"She's forced to show off her knowledge if she's asked specific questions. So would you if you were placed in that position."

"Louis," said Mrs. Miller, "why don't you let Mr. Penn explain?"

"Thank you," said Mr. Penn. "Mr. Miller, we're not used to such forward children in this school, or in this state."

"Jane has had a very good education. We read at home, too, and she's not used to holding back information if she's done her homework. Your school should be able to handle such bright students. There's a war on, you know, and more families will be coming from other parts of the country. They will be just as advanced as Jane."

"Perhaps she's a little bit bored," said Mrs. Miller. "Are you, Janie?"

"Well, I've had some of the lessons before, but you know, Mom, I can't do the math very well."

"Mr. Penn, how did you plan to punish Jane?" asked Mr. Miller.

Mr. Penn cleared his throat. "With a wooden paddle, sir. It's—"

"A *what*?"

"In the state of Texas we are allowed to use—"

"I don't give a damn about the state of Texas," shouted Mr. Miller as he jumped up. "Are you out of your mind? Show me that paddle right now!"

Mr. Penn held it up.

Mrs. Miller gasped and covered her eyes.

"Oh, my God, this is 1944, Mr. Penn, not the Middle Ages." Mr. Miller's voice rose even higher. "Now, listen to me, this is my daughter, my flesh and blood, and no one in this world—in this world—is going to lay a hand on her. Is that clear, Mr. Penn? Because if it is not very clear, I'll sue you and this entire school system if I have to."

"Mr. Miller, a paddling is only—"

"Didn't you hear me, sir? No one is going to touch or harm this child. We have *never* punished our children that way, and if you dare to try it, I'll name you as a perpetrator of a violent crime. Is that clear?"

"Yes," said Mr. Penn, "but you understand that she has to be dealt with in some way. I am also the principal of this school, and I have the right to—"

"I think we should take her home now, and we'll talk again later. We're all upset. Louis, sit down. Sit *down*!"

said Mrs. Miller. "Surely we can deal with this when we've all had a chance to think. Please, *please* put that paddle away, Mr. Penn!"

Mr. Miller took Jane's hands and gently pulled her to her feet. She suddenly realized she was very hungry. Her mother picked up her schoolbooks and the sodden paper lunch bag.

Mr. Penn held open the door. "I'm sure we can work out a solution," he said.

"Yes," replied Mr. Miller, "and in the meantime I suggest you burn that paddle."

As they passed through the outer office, Mrs. Wilcox whispered, "Good-bye, everyone." She reached out and touched Jane's shoulder.

School was almost over, and the breeze from the bay was stirring the banana trees and the beds of red and white roses on the lawn. Mr. Miller opened the door of the car. He turned and put his arms around Jane as Mrs. Miller arranged herself in the front seat. "You'll be all right, Janie," he said. "This will never happen again."

Chapter 2

J ane got into the backseat. "Daddy, where did you get this car?" The Millers' Chevrolet had long since given out, and there was no money to buy another.

"Mr. Bennett . . . you know, at my office—"

"He let you borrow it?"

"Well, darling, I didn't steal it." Mr. Miller frowned and cleared his throat.

"Oh, Daddy, I know . . ." Jane's skin prickled, and she squeezed her eyes shut. Jackass! she said to herself. Why did you say that? She knew that Daddy had done something wrong with other people's money and had been fired by his company in Chicago. That was why they had had to move.

One day last March Jane and her mother had met the landlord on the stairs. Softly he said, "Well, I see you have a lovely new fur coat, Mrs. Miller, but your husband

11

hasn't paid the rent in months. Maybe you should give me the coat instead."

For a moment Mrs. Miller didn't speak. She had clung to the banister. "What did you say, Mr. Wolfe?"

"Mr. Miller owes me a thousand dollars in back rent. And here you are in a new coat."

Mrs. Miller had clutched Jane's hand and sat down on the stairs. "I don't know what you're talking about, Mr. Wolfe, but I assure you my husband will contact you."

"He'd better—and soon."

When Mr. Miller came home that night there had been a terrible fight. "Is it true?" cried Mrs. Miller.

"Why do you believe everything you hear?"

"Don't lie to me. We're going to get thrown out. What have you been doing with all our money?"

Jane and Jeff peered into the living room from the foyer.

He whispered, "I've been spending it on the family. We are in . . . Ruth, I have done . . . something shameful."

Mrs. Miller ran to the phone and called her brothers, and they rushed over. "Please go to your rooms, children," said Uncle Mel. But while everyone was shouting and Mr. Miller was confessing, no one had noticed Jane and Jeff hidden behind the coat rack.

"Stole money from your own clients, Lou? How stupid can you be!" Uncle Burt hit Mr. Miller.

He staggered back and cried, "I didn't steal it. They were just insurance-policy dividends. I borrowed them. I was going to pay them back."

"When?" asked Uncle Burt as Uncle Mel held him

back. "When were you going to pay back those poor fools? In ten years, twenty years? How long have you been doing this?"

"Only a couple of years. People haven't been buying insurance since the war started. I had to do something." Mr. Miller touched his bloody cheek. He stared at his hand as if it belonged to someone else. "I'll pay back every last cent. I promise."

"You did the wrong thing, Lou," said Uncle Mel quietly. "You'll have to start all over now."

"I know, Mel. I'll find a way."

The insurance company had offered to give Mr. Miller one more chance: he could open an office in Corpus Christi. Now he was working to pay back all the money he had taken.

"Janie, are you listening to me?"

"Oh . . . yes, Daddy."

"What were you thinking about?"

"Nothing. I heard everything you said." Did he know what she had been remembering?

"Well, as I was saying . . . Mr. Bennett saw how upset I was. I wanted to get to your school quickly."

"That was nice of him." Jane looked at the back of his closely cropped head and knew she had been rescued. She wanted to reach over the front seat and put her arms around her father. She still didn't understand exactly what he had done in Chicago, but it always hung over her parents like one of those clouds above people's heads in the comic strips.

"You could have handled it better," said Mrs. Miller. "You always go overboard and embarrass me."

Mr. Miller wiped his forehead with his handkerchief. "That man is very peculiar. I had to stop him and I'll do it again if I have to."

"Peculiar?" asked Mrs. Miller.

"He likes swinging that weapon around, especially when it's going to be applied to little girls."

"You always exaggerate things," snapped Mrs. Miller.

"Daddy, what do you mean?"

Mr. Miller started. He had forgotten that Jane always listened.

"Oh, nothing, Janie . . . just that he gets carried away at times, that's all."

"Louis, you get carried away yourself."

"Is that so?" asked Mr. Miller.

Mrs. Miller shifted with irritation and looked out the window. Silence.

Why wasn't her mother happy that Daddy had rescued her? Jane concentrated on the road, lined with palm trees and oleander bushes in bright red-and-pink bloom. This was her favorite part of the ride home, Ocean Drive.

The vast expanse of the Bay of Corpus Christi was on their left. Fishing boats bobbed for the day's catch of shrimp. Gulf shrimp were huge and shaped like half moons and Texans ate them breaded in cornmeal and parsley and fried in deep, sizzling oil. Sharp blades of hunger flashed across Jane's stomach.

She looked out at mansions built by families who had made incredible fortunes in cotton and oil and cattle. There were Spanish homes with columns in front like Tara, Scarlett O'Hara's house in *Gone With the Wind*. Jane had just seen it at the movies.

Stone jockeys—Negro boys in bright clothes—held up lanterns at the entrances of many driveways. "Would it ever occur to any of them to paint those faces white instead of black?" her father would grumble almost every time they passed.

Long wooden piers stretched from the houses on the water side of the road. Sailboats and motor cruisers were anchored there. Lonely fishing poles, tilted in their fancy holders, waited for someone to come and cast their lines into the water. Mexican men in torn straw hats worked in the gardens.

At a sign, TOURIST COURT, they turned left from the road toward the water. Gravel hopped beneath the car as it stopped in front of a small stucco cabin. There were ten cabins. Each one had a long, narrow living room, a dark kitchen, two tiny bedrooms, a bathroom, and a little closetlike space. Mr. Miller used that room as an office.

Mr. Miller said that Shakespeare would have called this time for their family an "on-the-way scene." It certainly felt that way. In Chicago Jane's room had been decorated with flowered wallpaper and chintz curtains. The twin beds had white chenille spreads and pillows embroidered by her grandmother. Grandma was dead now, and the pillows and the furniture were in storage.

Jane got out of the car and looked at the gray-green bay. During the Chicago summers Jane's nurse, Margaret, had taken her to the beach on Lake Michigan in the mornings, where she had played with all her friends and their nannies. The clear blue water of Lake Michigan reflected the buildings and museum across the street. Then Margaret would take Jane home for a bath and a nap on her turned-down bed, the white sheets cooled by the rattling fan on the dresser.

Jane held the screen door of the cabin open for her mother.

"I'll be back at dinner," called Mr. Miller. "I have to return the car."

"Daddy, can I go with you?"

"MAY, Jane . . . *MAY."*

"MAY I go with you, please?"

"No, darling, forgive me . . . but I have to work. You can set the table and start your homework."

Jane ran back to the car. "But Daddy, I think Mom is really mad about today," she whispered. "Shouldn't I come with you just for a while?"

"No, honey . . . I said no."

"But Daddy—"

"No, Jane, now that's it." Little red veins appeared around his pupils, and Jane knew that she had gone too far.

In the kitchen Jane unpacked her books and threw the limp lunch bag into the wastebasket.

"Well, Jane, I guess you have to stay here with me." Her mother turned from the sink. "Sorry."

"Mother, I just wanted to—"

"You just wanted to get away from me. You've disgraced this family. I'm unbelievably ashamed."

"Mom, I—"

"Don't come near me."

Jane closed the door to her room and sat on the bed. She knew she should talk less in school if she wanted to be popular. Everyone always thought she was showing off.

But she just liked to study certain things. Not math and science, which made her shake. In Chicago the tutor had explained that she was just as smart as anyone, but that certain subjects, hard for her now, would get easier.

The long-division problems were like scratches when she looked at them. The left side seemed to go to the right, and then all the numbers moved across the page and left a ghost of themselves on the paper. Mr. Penn said, "Work harder, Miss Miller. If you're so smart, why can't you do this?"

"Jane," called Mrs. Miller, "Sally Garland is here to see you."

Jane leapt off the bed and went into the living room. Sally lived next door in a beautiful white clapboard house with green shutters and a glassed-in room that over-looked the bay. Jane and Sally often met on the beach below, but they had never been in each other's houses.

"Want to go down to the boat?" asked Sally.

Mrs. Miller smiled.

Suddenly Jane noticed her mother was a sweet and gentle person, almost purring because this little blond girl was standing on their stoop. Why wasn't her mother like that when they were alone—instead of crying, or shouting, or slamming the door behind her when she had been arguing with Jane's father?

The girls walked down to the beach. "Mr. Penn is a monster," said Sally as they waded into the shallow water.

Jane's face flushed with gratitude. "You're right. But my father came to school and yelled at him."

"He did?"

"Mr. Penn was going to paddle me."

"*Paddle* you?"

"He got out the paddle and everything."

"But he's never paddled a girl. Lots of boys, but my word! My father would be mad too."

"Have you ever seen that paddle?" asked Jane.

"Yes! Were you real scared?"

"Petrified."

"I don't blame you . . . you poor thing!"

Mr. Garland's motor boat was tied up at the dock. Sally and Jane climbed in and sat on one of the wooden seats. The little boat rocked back and forth in the choppy water.

"You know, Jane, everyone at school wants to like you, but you seem to be havin' . . . um . . . a lot of trouble."

"I know." Her face burned. Help was being offered. She was determined to accept it.

"Maybe," Sally said, "you could try to be just a little more . . . gentle. Know what I mean?"

"Maybe."

Jane looked at Sally's round brown face, topped by wispy, almost-white hair. Sally looked seriously at Jane. "Well, sometimes you make jokes that hurt people's feelin's because . . . I don't know . . . the kids don't understand them. You probably said things like that where you come from, but they just sound . . . um . . . kinda strong."

"Maybe," said Jane. If she had the right clothes and hair, no one would care what she said.

"I mean," continued Sally, "we know you're real smart. Your schools must be a whole lot better than ours, but you kind of keep remindin' us of that all the time."

At school Sally was always smiling and cheerful and surrounded by friends. She was the first one picked for volleyball or Red Rover or the softball team.

"What should I do?" asked Jane.

"Oh, gosh . . . I don't know. Just try to be . . . well, not so sarcastic maybe. I know you don't mean to be, but maybe you could just think a little bit about it."

Jane knew what she meant. Sometimes when the other girls were going to lunch together, Jane would feel so left out that she would say something, anything, to make them pay attention to her. It always came out sounding angry, but what she had meant to say was, Will you have lunch with me? Once on the playground she had hit Betty Lou Denison during a softball game, and she had no idea why. Everyone had comforted Betty Lou and gone on with the game. No one had spoken to Jane for the rest of the day.

The sun was disappearing as the girls climbed out of the boat, and Jane smelled night-blooming jasmine as they walked up the hill to the tourist court. Sea gulls plunged into the water, desperate for their evening meal, their bodies making tiny explosive fountains.

"Aren't those birds scary?" asked Jane. "What if one of them came after us?"

"They are," answered Sally, laughing, "but you're the only other person I ever heard say that! Let's run!"

From one of the cabins came the voice of a hillbilly group singing, "In the pines, in the pines, where the sun never shines. And it shivers when the cold wind blows . . ."

They ran until they reached the bushes near Sally's

house. "Want to come over and play tomorrow, Jane? It's Saturday and Josephine will make us pancakes for breakfast."

"In the pines, in the pines, where the sun never shines."

To play at Sally's! How would she act? What if she sounded like a *Yankee*? Would Sally's mother like her? She would wear her shorts and polo shirt. And no shoes.

"Yes, I'd like to," she said.

Chapter 3

That night there was lime Jell-O with grapes for dessert, Jane's absolute favorite, but she wasn't hungry. Jeff had been silent all through the meal. Mr. Miller finally said, "Jeff, what's bothering you?"

"Nothing, Dad."

"I know better, son."

"No, really . . . it's just . . ."

"Let's talk about it," said Mr. Miller. "You seem so unhappy."

"It's just that I've heard from some colleges."

"Which ones?" asked Mrs. Miller.

"Rice Institute, and SMU, and . . . uh . . . Harvard."

Jane's father turned pale. Beads of perspiration burst out on his face.

"What did Harvard say?" Mrs. Miller rose and leaned across the table toward Jeff.

"They've accepted me, Mother."

"Oh, Jeff, congratulations!" said Mrs. Miller, patting Jeff's cheek. And then, as if remembering something painful, she withdrew her hand and sat down quickly.

"Thanks, Mom, but really, I don't want to go. I know we can't afford it, and it's okay . . ."

"Perhaps we can find a way," said Mrs. Miller, looking at her husband.

Oh, that look that blamed Daddy for everything! Jane put down her spoon.

"Mom, I really don't have my sights set on college right now, not with the war on and everything."

"Of course you do," declared Mrs. Miller. "If your father really tries, you could go to Boston. It's such a wonderful place . . . and you were born there—"

"Ruth," Mr. Miller interrupted, "you know there's no way we can send Jeff to any college at all. We're barely surviving right now. Why do you encourage him?"

"But Daddy, couldn't Jeff get a scholarship?" asked Jane.

"Even if he did, Janie, he would still have to have transportation and money to live on, and we just don't have it," said Mr. Miller, clearing his throat. He tapped a fork on the table.

"Well, Lou, I could sell dresses or something."

"Ruth, I won't allow my wife to work. And even if I did . . . you just couldn't earn enough to make it worth your time."

"But it's wartime, Lou. A lot of women are working now. Don't be so old-fashioned."

"Ruth, I won't *hear* of it. Nobody we know has a wife who works. What would your father say?"

"Louis—"

"*No!* You should be here when Janie comes home from school."

"Dad . . . Dad, it's okay . . . honestly," said Jeff, his voice wavering. "Probably the only reason I got in was because of you. Alumni kids are always preferred."

"No, son, you were accepted because you are a top student and a swell kid." Mr. Miller brought his hands to his face and started to weep, at first quietly. Then his shoulders shook while great tears ran between his fingers and onto the blue-and-white tablecloth.

Jane began to cry, her hands twisting the material of her shorts. She wanted to go to her father and snuggle into his lap and comfort him. But that would make her mother mad.

"Jeff, I've always dreamed of your going to my school. I can't believe I can't send you there. I wish I could—you know that, don't you? You do know that?"

"Yes, Dad, I do . . . really. Please don't be so upset. It'll be fine. You know if I join the army, I could get the GI bill when I come out and go anywhere I want."

"No!" shouted Mrs. Miller, standing up and banging the table with her fist. "You are not volunteering. We've discussed this and discussed it, and we're not going to talk about it again."

"But—" said Jeff.

"*No!*" Mrs. Miller hit the table again.

"Mom, they're going to draft me anyway if I'm not in college."

"You are not going to enlist," said Mrs. Miller.

Jane reached down to pull up her socks. If only her mother would be still and let Jeff talk to her father.

"Dad, it's a 'good war'—you've said that yourself," said Jeff, "and I can do something about Hitler. Think what he's doing to the Jews."

"I thought Hitler was just invading places . . . you know . . . countries," said Jane. "What's he doing to the Jews?"

Silence.

"Nothing, Janie," said Jeff finally. "That is, we're not quite sure."

"But I heard you. It's a bad thing he's doing to the Jews, right? Otherwise you wouldn't all be looking like that."

"Jane," said Mrs. Miller, holding up her hand, "you're simply too young to understand, and it's better if we don't try to explain what we're not even sure of ourselves."

"Then you shouldn't say those things in front of me. Why do you do that when you know I'm sitting right here and can hear everything you say?"

"Jane," said Mr. Miller, "don't speak to your mother like that. If we choose not to tell you something, you must believe it's for your own good."

"But if Hitler is hurting the Jews in Europe, is he going to come over here and do the same thing to us?"

"No, of course not," said Jeff.

But did he mean it? Once in Chicago Jane had appeared in a temple play about something terrible done to the Jews, a *pogrom,* in a little town in Poland. Pogroms took place in Eastern Europe and in Russia. Jews had been attacked and killed by Christians, sometimes by their own Polish neighbors. Grandpa had often told her how his parents had been taken out of their house in Poland, and he had never seen them again. He had survived because he had hidden in a cabinet above the cookstove for two days.

Toward the end of the play—when the front door of her imaginary house had opened and the soldiers stormed in—Jane, playing the mother, had to say, "Oh, God, oh, God!"

"Speak up, Jane, we can't hear you," her teacher had said at every rehearsal. But people might laugh at her in the black babushka and the long, wrinkled skirt.

And the words, "Oh, God, oh, God," were so full of fear. If she actually said them, would something dreadful happen? Could the words bring a real pogrom to Chicago —into the lofty marble temple itself? If she just whispered, maybe it would never happen.

The day of the performance, with all the mothers and fathers and grandparents there, her heart had begun to race as the line approached. At the moment she was supposed to say "Oh, God, oh, God," she turned and muttered it, unheard, into the wooden ark which held the Torahs.

Could a pogrom take place right now in Corpus Christi? Her parents were afraid. Would Hitler come and take away her mother and father and Jeff? She shivered. What would she do? Who would take care of her? Would Grandpa come to get her, or would there be pogroms in

Chicago, too, and in Florida, where Aunt Libbie lived? Aunt Libbie and Uncle Seymour were old and sick. What if Hitler took over Miami Beach?

"Jane . . . Jane . . . did you hear me?"

"No, Mother. What?"

"I said we really don't know what is happening over there. Don't worry. Now clear the table, please. We won't talk about it anymore."

Jane took some plates into the kitchen. Was she supposed to sit there and pretend that she hadn't heard them? Did they think she was stupid? When she had children she would always tell them the truth and include them in her conversations. She would make them feel necessary and important. She banged the plates down on the counter and began to scrape. She had very good ideas of her own. Didn't anyone care what they were?

It was bad enough that Jeff was so handsome. Everyone made such a fuss over him and then said, "And your little girl . . . what a nice face she has." Jeff was perfect in school, and when he told his parents jokes Jane had to leave the room. She could hear them laughing and giggling. "Oh, Jeff, that's *disgusting*," her mother would say. "You shouldn't tell that story!" And then they would laugh again.

Jane dumped soap into the sink and turned on the water. She rattled the silverware, but she stopped when Jeff said, "Mother, please, we can't decide this right now."

"Yes, we can," said Mrs. Miller in a harsh whisper.

"But Daddy is upset. You know there are lots of kids like me, who don't have money for school. We're just coming out of the Depression, after all. Don't make him feel so bad. Let's wait until tomorrow."

"You are not going to enlist! Your father has got to find a way to send you to Harvard."

But there were many nights, even now, when their dinner was just cereal and milk. Each month when the owner of the tourist court came to the door for the rent, it was handed over carefully in a long white envelope.

At night Jane and Jeff would reach out between the twin beds and hold hands in the dark as they listened to their parents arguing.

"Louis, you have ruined our lives. I *hate* it here! I hate it!"

"Ruth, for God's sake, lower your voice. You'll wake the children. I'm working as hard as I can. Do you think I like the way we're living?"

"Then why did you get us into such trouble? Where was your brain?"

"Ruth, have a little pity—"

"I want my brothers, I want my family. They won't even write me anymore. You've taken them away from me!"

"This is a beautiful place."

"It's horrible."

"It's beautiful, I tell you. You just won't look. It has a great future and our lives will be better."

"It's *hot* and full of bugs and mildew, this smelly little house. You got us here and I could just kill myself."

"You helped get us here, Ruth."

"What?"

"You wanted cars and maids and furs. You decorated

the apartment over and over. There wasn't enough money. I got tired and did stupid things for you . . . stupid, yes! But—"

"Oh, of course, it's all my fault."

"I'm not saying that."

Jane heard a hairbrush smash against the wall. The bathroom door slammed. Then the click of the light switch and the sounds of the bedspread being whipped back.

Finally the house grew quiet. Jane and Jeff released their hands, turned over in their beds, and slept fitfully. Outside, the palm trees bent and struggled against the wind, and the waves lapped against the sand beneath the hill.

Chapter 4

A t nine o'clock the next morning Sally opened the door of her house. Jane saw shining wooden floors that seemed to sweep right out over the bay.

There were antique tables and chests smelling of lemon oil. The plump chairs and sofas were covered in soft green and blue. Vases of lilies and gardenias and roses were everywhere, and on the walls were oil paintings. Jane had never seen paintings like these outside of the Art Institute in Chicago: small, delicate scenes of sheep in green fields; churches with steeples rising into the clouds; women peeling vegetables in Dutch kitchens.

There were Oriental rugs in faded designs. Some had thin places where people had walked over them many times. Jane's mother would probably have thrown them away. She didn't like old things, not even the marble-topped, cherrywood furniture left to her by her own mother, Grandma Brodin.

"Ruth, we should at least take your mother's sideboard and the dressers," Mr. Miller had said one day when they were all sorting through Grandma's things with Grandpa. They were in the small Brodin apartment, which always smelled of pot roast and mothballs.

"Why? They're old and I wouldn't give them house room. Sorry, Papa, I don't mean to hurt your feelings," said Mrs. Miller.

"But they're beautiful, dear," said Mr. Miller, "and your brothers are taking some of it. That furniture is handmade—Jane and Jeff will inherit it someday."

"Just keep the night tables," said Grandpa. "Mama would be pleased."

"I know, Papa. But I'd rather have that new line at Marshall Field's. All easy to clean and the material is gorgeous. If you can't afford to buy new furniture, Lou, we'll just wait until later."

"Ruth," said Grandpa, "take Mama's tables and save your husband's money."

"Papa, it's all right," said Mr. Miller. "Ruth has different tastes from her mother, that's all. If she wants new furniture, I'll find a way to get it for her."

"Listen, Lou—"

"Let's not talk about it anymore," said Mrs. Miller as she folded a quilt and put it in a "give-away" box.

Jane had pretended to look at a photograph album. It would be nice to have the furniture. The white marble reflected the candles that Grandma lit every Friday night for *Shabbos*.

Now, in Sally's living room, she remembered that she had been looking at a picture of Mother and her two brothers when they were very little. Mother had an enormous black bow pulling back her straight, streaky-blond hair. Her white lace dress was immaculate.

A breeze blew in from the bay. How airy their apartment had been, with green plants in wicker stands in the living room. When Jane stood in the white entrance hall under the glittery chandelier she could look down the length of the apartment: white walls, rosy wallpaper, the swinging "service" door, and the yellow kitchen. Would she ever live in a clean, bright place again? A house with paintings and sunlight running across the floors?

"Sally, are you and your friend here hungry?" A young black woman carried an enameled tray into the room.

"Oh, Jo, this is my friend Jane," said Sally. "Jane, this is Josephine Wilson."

"How do you do, Jane. Now come on, girls. Eat over here and then you can go and play."

She set two places on a table near the windows, each with a plate of pancakes and a linen napkin standing upright. There were glasses of orange juice, a small pot of butter, and syrup in a pitcher with little ducks marching around the rim.

Jane had never seen pancakes like these: they were fluffy and shaped like fat pincushions. The juice had little bits of orange floating in it and was tart and light. It made her ears sting.

After they had eaten and returned the dishes to the kitchen, the girls sat on the floor and played Go Fish while, outside, gulls swooped and fighter planes flip-flopped through the clouds. Jane closed her eyes for a moment. How wonderful to be free—to swirl away over the choppy water to another place whenever you felt like it.

Josephine appeared again with an ice bucket, a bottle of Coca-Cola, a crystal goblet, and a package of Camel cigarettes.

"My mother's up," said Sally. "Pretty soon she'll call us to come in and talk to her."

How could anyone sleep so late in the heat? All the Millers were up early, before the little rooms became oppressive and still. But here it was cool and fresh.

"Children, where are you? Come in and keep me company," a raspy, hearty voice called.

"We're coming, Mama," said Sally. "Come on, Jane, this is the visitin' hour."

Sally led Jane down a short hall into a half-darkened room infused with the smell of perfume, soap, and cigarettes. The silver ice bucket glimmered on a bed table placed upon a pale pink quilt. A thin, smiling woman with mousy-brown hair leaned against lacy pillows. In her hand was a cigarette holder. It was made of gold and tortoiseshell. The smoke was weaving its way toward the French doors.

"So you're the famous Jane," said Mrs. Garland. "Welcome, Famous Jane. I hear you've just gotten here from Chicago. . . . What a fabulous city. Do you miss it?"

"Yes, ma'am."

"Goodness, what a jolt that must have been. And for your family too. . . . Goodness! Well, we certainly are a queer lot down here, wouldn't you say?"

"No, ma'am, not exactly—"

"Of course we are. It's the heat and the humidity . . . makes us all crazy. But I guess it's part of our charm. Sally, come over here, girl, and give me a hug."

Sally laughed and crawled onto the foot of the bed. Jane felt puffs of air escape from the quilt, making the curtains billow gently from their carved wooden poles.

As Sally hugged her mother Jane leaned forward and looked at the silver-framed pictures on the table: men in cowboy hats and boots and women in long dresses. Behind them were log cabins with cows grazing near scrubby mesquite trees. In other pictures the same people, older now, were standing in front of great mansions or country houses with aisles of trees leading up to the front porches. Some of the men, bushy-bearded and gray, were on horseback, the silver decorations on their carved saddles flashing.

There were photographs of Sally in a long white christening dress; as a flower girl at a wedding; sitting on her father's lap at a barbecue and holding her mother's hand at the edge of a swimming pool, one strap of her suit falling over her sloping shoulder.

"What does your daddy do? Does he like it here?"

"He sells insurance, Mrs. Garland. And yes, ma'am, he does like it. He says there's always a breeze, no matter how hot it gets."

"Well, he's right about that. But the breeze feels a lot better if you have a gin and tonic in your hand. Or at least a Coke. Sally darlin', run and ask Jo to bring me another one, would you? This one is gone, gone, gone."

Sally left the room and Jane stared at Mrs. Garland.

Could this be a mother? Mrs. Garland laughed a hoarse whinny as she pushed back the collar of her bed jacket. "I stay up all night readin'. If I'm not dancin' at the club, and then I sleep till noon and have a breakfast of Cokes and cigarettes. Anyone you know in Chicago ever do that?"

"No, ma'am."

"See? Proves my point exactly. We're all very, very strange. But don't worry, you'll love it here. It's a fine place to grow up, although I must say our school system leaves somethin' to be desired."

"Oh, no, ma'am."

"Oh, yes . . . yes, indeed. We all know that and we're tryin' to do something about it. Schools up north teach subjects a lot earlier than we do."

"Mr. Penn thinks I'm just—"

"Oh, *that* one. Hmm. Just give it a little time. You'll be a happy girl, you'll see. Sally says you're smart as paint and that you're the best dodgeball player they've got."

"She does?" asked Jane. Then she noticed a collection of little objects on a round table in the corner of the room.

"You want to have a look at those nonsenses, Jane? Go right ahead and touch everythin'. They're just for fun."

Jane bent over the table. It was like a museum! China boxes and enameled eggs; glass and filigreed elephants, cats, even dogs sitting up to beg. She picked up a china fox. It made a cool spot in the palm of her hand.

Sally and Josephine entered the room and while Mrs. Garland was pouring her Coke, Josephine drew back the curtains and opened the glass doors even farther. On the terrace outside were buckets of roses and geraniums. The banisters were covered with thick wisteria and night-blooming jasmine, closed tightly now.

Mrs. Garland, her diamond ring dancing in the sun, lit another Camel, blew out the match, and said, "All right, little girls, I'm facin' my day. I'm going to bathe now and get down to the drugstore for lunch. What are you goin' to do?"

"We're probably goin' to the beach, Mama, and maybe do some crabbin' off the dock."

"Sounds good, hon. But no swimmin' unless there's a grown-up there, hear?"

"Yes, ma'am," replied Sally, "but we won't go in, anyway, because there are tons of jellyfish today. Jo said she saw a man o'war this mornin'."

"Oh, God," said Mrs. Garland. "Stay out of that ghastly water."

And goblet in hand, surrounded by circles of smoke, she vanished into the pink-and-white bathroom.

Chapter 5

The following Monday was Rosh Hashanah, the Jewish New Year. Jane looked into her closet.

"Mother, can I wear my dress with the lace sleeves?"

"No, the brown wool skirt and a blouse."

"Mom, I'll die of the heat!"

"Nice people don't wear white after Labor Day."

"But—"

"That's enough."

In Chicago, for "erev" Rosh Hashanah, the evening that begins the New Year, Mrs. Miller had always worn a new dress and new coat, and a hat with a little veil over her bright blue eyes. On the first night of the service Mr. Miller wore a stiff new suit with a vest and a printed silk tie. The next morning, on New Year's Day, the suit had wrinkled and softened to fit his short, powerful shape, and the tie was twisted.

In their new clothes Jane and Jeff had sat in the soaring marble temple filled with Indian-summer light. All around them were aunts and uncles and friends. Not Grandpa, of course. Their temple was Reform, and Grandpa was at his Orthodox shul. Jane had gone there once with Grandma. The women had to sit upstairs and no music was allowed, just the chanting of the black-coated men swaying back and forth as their tallises, the long silk scarves, waved like dancers' costumes. But at her own temple everyone sat together and there was an organ, sometimes even a violin or a harp. In the last moments of Rosh Hashanah, the rabbi lifted the shofar, the curved ram's horn, and blew three times. It sounded like shepherds and hills in Jerusalem and old, smoky synagogues of long ago.

"Daddy, why does the rabbi's face get so red when he blows the shofar?" she had asked years earlier.

"It's a difficult instrument, honey . . . very primitive. It takes a lot of breath."

"I always get goose bumps when he does it."

"I do too, Jane . . . it signifies a new beginning . . . a new year to try again to—"

"To be a better person?"

"Yes, to be a better person," he had said, looking away.

Afterward all the Miller relatives had come to Jane's house for a feast. There was chopped liver and chicken and green salad and pickles and sauerkraut, challah bread and all kinds of cakes and cookies covered with powdered sugar that ended up in lacy patterns on the floor.

Some of the relatives were very poor and lived in dark, small apartments. Mrs. Miller loved to feed them all and give them food in waxed-paper packages to take home and eat later. She gave Jane's cousins new blouses and socks and toys. Once Jane saw her mother giving Aunt Tilly a brand-new dress. "No, Ruth, it's too expensive," Aunt Tilly had said. But Mrs. Miller replied, "You look much better in it than I do" as Aunt Tilly slipped the dress into her pocketbook.

Now it was September in Corpus Christi, and the Millers, in a borrowed car, were on their way to the temple for the first time. The rabbi had been to see them a few weeks earlier, but he would be busy tonight. He might not even say hello. What if no one spoke to them? Would they know where to sit? They didn't have new clothes this year. Would they look shabby?

They parked under a banana tree. The white stucco building looked like an old Spanish mission. Rough wooden beams extended from the roof, and the stained-glass windows were deep-set and small. Palm trees and gardenia bushes were everywhere on the thick spiky grass, and all was still in the twilight. As the Millers walked up the path toward the heavy wooden door, the smell of the flowers rose in little clouds under Jane's shoes.

"Well, Mr. Miller, this is your family?" asked a tall man in a light suit. His voice boomed out over the crowd.

"Yes, indeed, Mr. Goldberg," said Mr. Miller, and introduced them.

"Nice to have ya'll with us."

A Jewish man with a Texas accent! And Mrs. Goldberg had a Texas accent too. "Ya'll sure enough must feel strange your first Rosh Hashanah down heah in Corpus. So happy you've joined our little temple."

"Thank you," said Mrs. Miller, looking amazed at the welcome. "We're glad to be here too."

"We'll have to set up a special Sunday-school class for Janie here," said Mrs. Goldberg. "Maybe we'll put her up one grade. Honey, we have the little bitty ones and the teenagers, but nobody in between. Don't you worry, though. More and more people are movin' in all the time."

Everyone was talking and slowly filing into the temple. A willowy, dark woman with her hair pulled tightly into a knot at her neck was greeting people at the entrance. She was the most beautiful person Jane had ever seen.

"You must be the Millers," she said with a French accent as she held out her hand. "I am Dede, Rabbi Schuman's wife. Welcome! Welcome!" Jane stared at the tiny round diamonds in her ears. They were pierced! Mother said that nice people didn't have pierced ears. But Mrs. Schuman looked as if she should be in a magazine. How did a French person happen to be here?

"Thank you," said Mr. Miller, beaming down at Jane and Jeff. "We've heard wonderful things about you."

Mrs. Schuman laughed. "Ah, no, no. Lies, lies . . . all of them lies. Drive them from your mind! Where would you like to sit?"

"Is there a seating plan?" asked Mrs. Miller, adjusting her collar.

"None at all. But the music sounds best if you sit up front."

Inside the temple people were arranging themselves in pews. In Chicago there had been velvet seats, but pews were much more fun. Some of the women, in straw hats and cool dresses, were speaking softly to one another as they removed their short white gloves. The men wore pale suits and string ties. The Millers' Chicago clothes were out of place. Only Jeff, tall and handsome, seemed comfortable. People were glancing at him and whispering. Jane turned to him too. When had he started looking like a grown-up?

Organ music spilled out from a loft over the doorway. "It's Bach," whispered Mr. Miller. "Isn't that a treat?" Soon a large man in a full white robe entered the loft and began to arrange music on a stand. It was Mr. Dretzin, the plumber. He had fixed their sink! Was he going to sing?

The rabbi took his seat on the pulpit. Above the ark, which held the Torahs, was the red eternal light, the *ner tamid,* which symbolizes the presence of God in the temple. It never goes out. In Chicago it had been housed in a fancy gold holder, but here it was a simple red light on a thin brass chain. Back home the soot had settled on all the windowsills and niches and decorations, but the rough white walls of this temple were bare and clean.

On one side of the pulpit were three flags in brass holders: the American flag, the red, white, and blue Texas flag, and a white silk flag with the Star of David rippling in the center.

"Lou, why do they have the Texas flag, for God's sake?" whispered Mrs. Miller.

Mr. Miller laughed. "State pride runs high everywhere. Kind of nice, don't you think?"

"It's ridiculous." Mrs. Miller took off her gloves. "They can't be serious."

Jane thought the Jewish flag, in this building like a Mexican fortress, was the odd one. The blue Magen David, the Star of David, was lonely against its plain white background. The other two flags, boldly colored and heavier, were at home.

Jane had always wanted to wear the six-pointed Magen David on a chain around her neck, but her mother had said, "Nice people don't wear them."

"Why not, Mother?"

"Because it's proclaiming who you are. It's like saying, I'm different. As when Christians wear crosses. It's protesting too much."

Jane frowned. It would be nice to have that shiny star on a delicate little necklace. Then people would know more about you. It would be easier to make friends here. Or would it? Wearing a cross was probably easier. Then no one would ask any strange questions.

As the service began, it was funny to hear Hebrew read with a drawl. Mr. Miller winked over the children's heads at Mrs. Miller, but she looked forward primly.

"I saw your mother walking across the Sherry Hotel lobby in Chicago," Daddy used to say. "She was the loveliest girl I had ever seen—silky blond hair and a slim little figure—and I made up my mind to meet her."

"What did you do?" Jane loved to ask the question each time the story was told.

"My aunt Carol, who was with me, knew her and arranged an introduction."

"Did you propose right away?"

"No, I was too frightened. She was shy and quiet, and here I was—this football player from Boston. I didn't think she'd have me. Besides, she was still in college. How could I ask her to quit and marry me?"

"But she did! She did!"

"She did . . . lucky for me. Because now I have you and Jeff too."

But nowadays it was hard to think of her as that girl in the gilt lobby of the Sherry Hotel. Daddy had always said, "She wore a light pink dress with short sleeves and lace around the neck." Maybe Jane would ask Daddy to tell the story again on the way home.

Sitting between her father and Jeff, she felt protected and safe. Mr. Miller sometimes wiped his eyes with his handkerchief, especially when the prayer for the dead was recited. He was remembering his father and mother.

Mr. Dretzin's baritone voice was just like an opera singer's, but the melodies were not the same as those in Chicago. Jane's favorite song was "May the Words":

> *May the words of my mouth,*
> *And the meditations of my heart,*
> *Be acceptable*
> *In Thy sight, O Lord,*
> *My rock and my redeemer.*
> *Amen.*

She had always sung it with confidence. Now she pretended to sing, but when they came to the words "be acceptable in Thy sight, O Lord," she gave up and closed the book. Did God think that she didn't have "meditations of the heart" just because she had learned a different melody in another place? Was He looking down now at her and wondering why she wasn't singing?

After the rabbi's benediction everyone said, "Happy New Year," or *"L'Shana Tovah."* People leaned over the pews and shook hands or embraced. Mr. and Mrs. Miller kissed each other and then put their arms around Jane and Jeff. "Happy New Year, Jane," said Mrs. Miller. "A good year, son," said Mr. Miller, kissing Jeff's cheek.

Jeff hugged Jane quickly. "May you be inscribed forever, kiddo—"

"—in the Book of Life," she said. They laughed and lightly punched each other's shoulders.

On the steps of the temple, lighted by yellow lamps in brass holders, everyone spoke to the Millers. The soft night, under a starry black sky, folded itself around them and all these people who read the Torah and sang different tunes and sounded like the prairies and the movies.

Rabbi Schuman took Mrs. Miller's hand. "Can you get here for Yom Kippur? If not, we'll arrange a car for you." He smiled at Jane and laid a hand on her shoulder. Behind his glasses, his eyes looked right into hers, as if she were the only person standing there.

"Well, thank you. We'll call you if we have any trouble," replied Mrs. Miller.

"Mrs. Miller, I am Adele Perlberger," said a small woman. "My husband and I wanted so much to invite you over, but you don't have a telephone."

"We do now."

"Well, that's lovely. May I call you?"

"Yes, please do." Mrs. Miller was smiling. Jane moved closer to her. Some of her mother's calm seemed to wrap around her too. Mrs. Miller listened intently to Jeff as he spoke to the rabbi. Jane felt peaceful. Maybe now her mother would like it here.

In the car the moon poured through the windows, shadowing Jane's legs with stripes. She looked around through her fingers, framing pictures. Jeff's face was glowing. Her father put his arm along the back of the seat, almost touching her mother's shoulder. Mrs. Miller was silent.

Tomorrow they would go back to the temple for the last service. It was a new year, and things would get better now.

Chapter 6

Grandpa had made his first visit to Corpus Christi after Yom Kippur in October. For the first few days he had been in shock. There were too many churches. It was too hot. The temple was too far away. No cronies to chum around with, and no one to buy the ties and handkerchiefs and belts he sold for a living.

Two days after his arrival Jane was hanging out the wash and Grandpa was holding the clothespins, when Mr. Leigh, their neighbor, sat down on his tiny front porch and began untying knots in his fishing line. "Hello, honey, and . . . Sir." He nodded to them.

"Mr. Leigh, this is my grandfather, Leon Brodin. He's visiting us from Chicago."

Grandpa, in his dusty suit and walrus mustache, bowed. Mr. Leigh said, "How do you do, sir," and began to pick at a knot.

"My pleasure, Mr. Leigh. I see you are preparing to go fishing."

"I'm goin' out on my boat. Would you like to come along and cast a line?"

"No, thank you," answered Grandpa.

"It'll be a good dinner tonight . . . I'm goin' for crab."

Grandpa shuddered slightly and said, "No, thank you, sir . . . I am not a man of the sea."

"Going on the boat would be so much fun," said Jane, after Mr. Leigh had gathered up his fishing gear and disappeared down the stone stairs to the beach. "Why couldn't you have said yes? He's a nice man, Grandpa."

"I'm sure he's a very pleasant person, Jane. But I want nothing to do with crabs or shrimp—*traife*. You know shellfish are forbidden to Jews. Shellfish eat anything and everything in the sea. Terrible scavengers!"

"But Grandpa—"

"They have no discrimination."

"But Grandpa, you could just—"

"Besides, I don't like boats."

"Why didn't you tell him that in the first place?"

"I didn't want to hurt his feelings."

"But I think you hurt his feelings anyway."

"No, Jane, I'm sure I didn't. I'm an old Jewish man. People forgive old Jewish men lots of things."

"You could have just watched, Grandpa."

"I'm sure fishing or, God forbid, crabbing, might be enjoyable," he admitted. "But that world and mine are different. And you're not part of that world either."

"Grandpa, I'd like to have a *little* part of this world. I don't have a best friend here. Not yet anyway."

"You have other things, Jane. You're a descendant of Abraham and Sarah. Your people have survived slavery in Egypt and pogroms in Poland. Friends are not as important as living a life of dedication."

"*Grandpa!* How can you say such a thing?"

"I can say anything I like. I am an old Jewish man."

Jane had finished hanging the laundry, and the clothes and linens whipped around the line like sails caught in a hurricane. The wind almost blew away the empty basket, but Grandpa reached for it and handed it back.

"Thank you," she said, frowning.

"Jane, how about a walk on the beach?"

"Are you going to lecture me some more?"

"I make no promises."

"Okay. I guess so. But *try* not to lecture me."

"We'll see. Take the basket in and get me a sweater, please."

The beach curved left into a little cove marked by rocks that formed a shallow pool when the tide was out. Jane waded into the water, and Grandpa took off his high-top black shoes and socks and carefully placed them on the sand. Then he rolled up his trousers, exposing his thin white legs. He held the pants up at the knees and carefully walked to join Jane in the middle of the clear pool.

"I'm sorry if I upset you before, Janie."

"About being different?"

"Yes. The fact is that your background is not the same as that of most of the people here. You live in a strange place with a strange name."

"Corpus Christi?"

"*Oy!* 'Body of Christ,' " moaned Grandpa, clutching his head.

"Oh, sorry, Grandpa, but I didn't choose the name—"

"It's not just the name, Jane. It seems to me that you're forgetting what it is to be a Jew. It is the best thing in the world. We are closer to God than any other people."

"My friends think they are close to God too."

"They have their Jesus Christ standing between them and God. We speak directly to God. We don't have a go-between."

"But they love their Jesus—"

"Don't tell me. I know that! But he is not the messiah! Our messiah is still to come!"

"But Grandpa, look how long we've been waiting for him."

"Jane! I'm ashamed of you. The wait is not long if you live your life fully as a practicing Jew. God chose the Jews and we're a people steeped in beauty and tradition and law. We are a people of *law,* little girl."

"Oh, you mean kosher laws and things, and—"

"I mean laws for living, for praying, for eating, for getting along with our neighbors. It's all very complicated and interesting and more difficult than being a Christian, I can tell you. And it's all filled with God's love."

"I *know* it's more difficult, but my friends have all kinds of complicated holidays and customs too."

"I'm sure they do, but it's not good for you to associate with them."

"Grandpa, I have to LIVE here!"

"They can influence you and corrupt you."

"You take that back! Sally is my friend. She likes me."

"She may like you very much, but Christians are dedicated to converting Jews to their religion and you have to be wary. You can be polite to her, but you must maintain your independence."

"I can't believe you're saying this to me."

"It's only because I love you so much, Janie. I want you to grow up and be God's child and have Jewish children of your own who will live good lives. Don't you understand that?"

"I'll be friends with anyone I want to. You don't understand anything about this!"

"You will find out, Jane. . . ."

Jeff ran toward them. "Hi! Anyone want to go in the water with me?" He waved his towel like a lariat.

"No, thanks," said Jane, trying not to cry. How could Grandpa be so stubborn? "Too many jellyfish in the water."

"Oh, don't be a scaredy-cat," said Jeff, plunging into the pool and splashing water in all directions.

"Jeff, it's *cold*!" said Jane, holding her arms against her chest. Grandpa stepped elegantly away and brushed the drops from his clothing.

"Grandson, a little less wild, please."

"Well, what are you talking about, then?" Jeff asked as he gazed longingly at the bay. There was a family rule about not swimming alone.

"I don't want to talk about it anymore," said Jane.

"You're talking about how much Grandpa hates Corpus Christi."

"Oy!" groaned Grandpa.

"Oh, sorry, Grandpa," said Jeff. "Didn't mean to hurt your feelings. Why don't we talk about something else?"

"Tell us about Grandma and the boat," said Jane.

"But you've heard it a hundred times," said Grandpa, although he was clearly winding up to spin the tale.

"Well, tell it anyway," said Jane.

"Well, let's see . . . Your great-grandmother and great-grandfather brought over to this country seven children in steerage, and one of those children was my wife-to-be, Martha."

"Our grandmother," said Jeff.

"Yes, your grandmother. She was just ten years old. It was a terrible journey in the bottom of the ship, with no privacy and very little sanitation."

"Right," said Jane.

"And the ship finally docked," said Grandpa, "and the family thought they were in New York, but the truth is that they were in Canada—"

"—because the agent had sold them the wrong tickets," said Jeff.

"Exactly," replied Grandpa after a slight pause.

"Sorry, Grandpa," Jeff said. "I get carried away."

"So they waited and waited, but no one came to meet them," said Grandpa. "And the officials wouldn't let them get off the ship—"

"—and no one had eaten for days and days—"

"Jane! Are you going to let me tell this?"

"Yes, Grandpa." Jane put her hand over her mouth.

"Thank you. Well, now . . . uh . . . the baby was crying . . . and the children were practically starving because all the kosher food had been eaten days before. So Great-grandma Woldenberg told your grandmother, Martha, to see if someone would let her go and look for decent food."

"And it had been days since she had been on solid ground, so she felt very strange." Jane could not resist.

Grandpa sighed. "Yes, Jane. Now, she didn't speak a word of English, but eyes wide and stomach growling, she peered into all the stands and barrels. And finally she saw some brown-and-yellow fruit . . . at least she thought it might be fruit—"

"—and they were covered completely by their own skins, so she thought they could possibly be kosher," Jeff said, and held up his hands as if to ward off a blow.

"Oh, all right, you finish, then," said Grandpa, sulking.

"No, no, you finish . . . please. I apologize," said Jeff, smiling quickly at Jane.

Grandpa cleared his throat dramatically and said, "Martha wanted to buy the odd-looking fruit, but she had no money. The vendor said that he would take the thin wire of gold around Martha's wrist—her only piece of jewelry—and the little girl knew she had to do it."

"Oh, brave Martha," said Jane.

"Yes, brave Martha. Your grandmother was a very strong woman. And she gave the bracelet from Poland to the man for—"

"—five bunches of bananas. And the Woldenberg family was saved!" cried Jane. Grandpa smiled and Jeff yelled

"Hooray!" as he threw his arms up like a football hero to honor the victory of his grandmother.

"Thank you, Grandpa, I love that story," said Jane.

"Oh, you children are very rude . . . very rude," he answered, but he hugged Jane hard and shook Jeff's chin in feigned anger. "Very bad. I'll never tell you another family story."

"Oh, yes, you will!" said Jeff.

"Yes," grumbled Grandpa, "I'm sure I will."

Two fighter planes were doing somersaults in the air as the three walked back toward the tourist court. Jane, wrapped in Jeff's towel, looked for beach glass as Jeff ran in knee-high water. Grandpa took out his prayerbook and put on his glasses. Occasionally he would stop, move his lips, and shake his head in wonder, as if this were the first time he had ever read the words.

Chapter 7

In November Jane was transferred to a new English class. The teacher, Mrs. Creighton, taught about the Greeks and Romans and their plays and the way their theaters were built, their clothes and drinking vessels and plates and sandals and writing materials. She showed slides and rushed up and down the aisles as each new picture appeared.

"Ah, children, look at the brilliance of this architecture," she cried as she pointed at the screen. "Imagine the people who lived in these places!"

Mrs. Creighton was almost as strict as Mr. Penn, but Jane felt swept along by her wild energy. Other classes were harder. Jane was still behind in math and science.

Sally and Jane played together more and more and sometimes did homework together. Now Jane sat in the lunchroom with Sally's friends, and the other girls didn't ask so many questions about her life up north. Still, she always felt slightly left out. They had all grown up together.

Late in November the palm trees began to shed their bottom branches. The brown, twisted leaves lay on the ground, and for the first time Jane wore a sweater to school.

"Baruch ata Adonai Elohainu melech ha'olam asher kidshanu . . ." Jane's mother, a lace kerchief covering her hair, said the prayers over the sabbath candles. The flames cast their light across the Friday night tablecloth, with its appliquéd birds and leaves and trailing flowers sewn by someone's meticulous hands in a far-away Polish village. Great-grandma Woldenberg had brought it to America in the hold of the ship. It was one of the few things not sold to pay for their passage.

". . . borai pri hagafen . . ." Mr. Miller held up the silver kiddush cup and recited the prayer for the wine. "Who creates the fruit of the vine," the words said.

A blue Wedgwood bowl, saved from Chicago, held oranges in the center of the table. It was engraved with a ring of white figures, like icing on a cake. People dressed in old-fashioned clothes held hands as they solemnly walked around the bowl. When she was small, Jane had wondered if they ever actually got around to the side they were not on, the side they never saw. She liked to think they had happy reunions in the middle of the night, in the dark corner kitchen cabinet, where the bowl was kept all week, wrapped in its cloth.

Jeff recited the prayer over the challah bread. Everyone said "Amen," and then he tore off a piece of the braided loaf and passed it to each person.

This was a particularly good dinner because Jane's father had sold a large policy to a department store in town. There were lamb chops, wedges of lettuce covered with French dressing, little crispy, round potatoes, broccoli, and carrots. Jane liked the vegetables better than the meat, but her mother made a fuss when she didn't eat all the food on her plate, so she finished everything.

There was pound cake with canned fruit for dessert, and her father even let her taste the sweet red wine. She made a face and everyone laughed. Why did grown-ups like wine so much, and Scotch and whiskey? When she grew up she would never drink those things, only juice and milk shakes and iced tea with mint leaves and lemon in frosty glasses.

Jane clamped her toes around the rung of her chair and took a deep breath. "Uh . . . Mommy, Daddy . . . Sally asked me to come to her Christmas party. They're going to trim their tree and—"

"They're going to trim a *tree*?" asked Mrs. Miller as she put her fork down with a clank. "What would your grandfather say? A Jewish girl trimming a tree? Of course you can't go."

"Mom, why does he have to know?" asked Jeff. "He's in Chicago. This doesn't have anything to do with Grandpa."

"But you know he's coming for Chanukah," answered Mrs. Miller.

"But that's after the party, isn't it? When's the party, Janie?" asked Jeff.

"Sunday night."

"It's not at all appropriate for Jane to be there," said Mrs. Miller, a tinny edge to her voice. "We have a tradition to uphold. We have our own holiday, and there's never been a member of my family who has ever had anything to do with a Christmas tree."

"But Mom," said Jeff, "it's only this once."

"You know perfectly well that Jewish people don't participate in the celebration of Jesus' birth," Mrs. Miller said firmly. "We celebrate the miracle of saving the Temple and the survival of the Jewish people."

"Ruth," said Mr. Miller, adjusting his yarmulke, "she won't be breaking a tradition by hanging a colored ball on a pine tree, for God's sake. What's wrong with you?"

"Did you ever go to a party like that, Daddy?" asked Jane.

"Oh, once. The boys in my dorm at college threw a shindig in the lobby . . . ah . . ."

Jeff cleared his throat and looked with great concentration at his spoon.

Mr. Miller's eyes grew sad.

"Oh, God, Louis," said Mrs. Miller, hunching her shoulders and leaning forward on the table.

"I'm sorry, son," said Mr. Miller, his voice barely audible. "So sorry."

"It's okay, Dad. Don't be afraid to talk . . . please."

There was a long pause.

Jane wanted to cry out, It'll be all right. Please, everyone, tell me that it will be all right. She wanted to hug her brother and kiss her father's cheek. For a moment she could feel herself taking Jeff's hand and placing it into her father's trembling one, so they would embrace and everything would be better

She didn't want Jeff to go to Europe and be hurt by Hitler. She wanted the war to end and their furniture to be sent from Chicago. She wanted her chenille bedspreads and her little pillows. She wanted just one homemade cotton dress. She wanted to run barefoot and have calluses on her feet. She wanted to ride a horse easily and learn to say "paper sack" instead of "paper bag" and "picture show" instead of "movie house." But most of all she wanted this family to stop being so miserable.

"So, please, may I go to this party or not?"

"Yes, you may go," said Mr. Miller.

"*Louis!*" Mrs. Miller's voice grew even harder.

"She's *going*," said Mr. Miller at the same moment Jeff shouted, "Mom, leave her alone. Why are you so hard on her?"

"You're both against me. Well, take her side—what do I care? You're wrong and my father will tear his shirt, as if she were dead. But that's fine, just fine. Do whatever you want."

"Your father will not tear his shirt," said Mr. Miller.

"He will. He *will*! If he finds out what she is going to do, he will think of her as dead. You *know* he's an Orthodox Jew, and he'll declare her gone from this world and tear his shirt if he thinks she has committed sacrilege by honoring Jesus Christ. Why do I have to explain this?"

"Daddy, it's all right. Never mind," said Jane.

"No, it's not all right," said Mr. Miller. "If your grandfather is going to be that extreme, let him. You have a right to live your own life. You are going to the party!"

Mrs. Miller rose from her chair, went to the bedroom, and shut the door. They heard her sobbing. It seemed far away, as if she had put the pillow over her mouth.

Chapter 8

The Garland tree was the tallest one Jane had ever seen—not counting the one at Marshall Field's in Chicago. As the last rays of bright orange light flooded through the French doors, boxes of ornaments, tinsel, ribbons, and strings of twisted lights were placed near the tree. Carols were playing. A wide silver bowl of eggnog stood on a sideboard beside plates of cookies and sandwiches. The Garlands' friends, dressed in cool cotton clothes, introduced themselves to Jane. "How do you like it here in Corpus?"

"Very much, thank you."

"Of course you do. It's the best-kept secret in the United States of America, wouldn't you say? Isn't this the best little city in the U.S. of A.?"

"Yes, it is." Did they know she had never been to such a party?

Other girls from school were there too: Sarah Jane,

Mary, Betty Gay, Janet, Billy Joyce, Joan, and Patty Rose. They all wore shorts with sharp, starched creases, and polo shirts. So did Jane. They had fresh ribbons on the ends of their braids, and Jane had clipped a yellow barrette into the side of her hair. No one wore shoes.

Jane loved putting the little hooks into the ornaments and finding the perfect place to hang them. There were twirling tin sticks that danced when the air moved, miniature Santa Clauses in old-fashioned red suits, stars dusted with sequins, handmade quilted houses and squares, and shiny balls with country scenes outlined in white frosty paint.

There were real candy canes, string bags of red-hots that burned the mouth, gold-covered chocolate money, enameled camels and donkeys, and papier-mâché men holding walking staffs in their tiny hands, their heads wrapped with scarves. They must be the Three Wise Men who had gone to see the baby Jesus.

And here she was—putting one of them in the middle of a long, drooping branch. Should a Jewish girl be honoring these men who brought gifts to Jesus Christ?

"When do we get our own messiah, Grandpa?" she had asked once.

"When God so wills it—that's when we get him."

"But when do you *think* it might be, Grandpa?"

"I have no idea, Janie, but in the meantime we live our lives as good Jews and enjoy every day. Dance and sing, and the messiah will find you."

Mr. Garland climbed up a ladder to the top of the tree and attached an ice-blue angel, her wings spread wide and transparent. Was there really a heaven? Grandpa had said, "Heaven is here on earth and is measured in the service we give to others, and we should treasure all the moments of our lives." But the angel, in her halo of shining rhinestones, had a knowing, secret smile on her face.

And hell too. The kids at school talked a lot about hell. They learned about it at their churches, which they talked about all the time: the Church of the Good Shepherd, the First Baptist Church, the Linden Presbyterian Church, the Community Methodist Church. Not so much the Catholic Church. Only Flora May Simpson went there, and the other girls hardly ever asked her to play or to eat with them.

Someone plugged in the lights, and the tree was suddenly a dazzling, shimmering melody of color and sparkling beams of light that struck every corner of the room.

"Ahhhhh, isn't it a beauty?"

"Good grief, what a tree! What a tree!"

Applause. Everyone spoke at once. The grown-ups kissed the children.

"Get out the camera, Henley," said Mr. Garland to his wife. "We need this one in the history book."

"Wait, Daddy, let's turn out all the other lights first," cried Sally, and all the girls ran around the room, clicking off the lamps and the chandelier.

Mrs. Garland placed a cup in Jane's hand. It tasted of cinnamon and nutmeg—like a milk shake made of cream. It was delicious and not strong at all. Would Grandpa be angry if he found out that she had tasted eggnog?

Mr. Garland began to play Christmas carols on the piano. People drifted over and sang "Silent Night," and "The First Noel," and an unfamiliar one Jane particularly loved, called "Good King Wenceslas." Grandpa would really tear his shirt. She sang loudly, but when the words "Christ" or "Jesus" came up, she put her lips together and lowered her head so that no one could see her. If the messiah was really looking for her, she didn't want to ruin her chances completely.

Chapter 9

M
r. Garland's pickup truck, black and rusted from the salt air, was big enough for only two people to ride in front, so Jane and Sally shared the passenger seat and seemed to be one body, with an arm on each side, their inner arms in back, and four legs with two sets of sneakers. This two-headed creature squealed and yelled as the truck hit the ruts and holes on the road leading to Mr. Garland's cotton farm a few miles inland from the bay.

This is my friend, thought Jane. And my shirt is like hers, and my shorts are almost like hers, and we both have on sneakers, and my hair is getting longer.

Last night she had decorated a tree for the very first time in her life, and today felt as if she were a ball of twine unwinding . . . unwinding from the little house by the water, from the moment each day when her mother would go to the mailbox to see if Jeff's draft notice had come.

Here in the country were cotton fields and greenish ponds, with donkeys and sheep and horses grazing nearby. Working oil pumps, scattered throughout the fields, were moving up and down like great metal giraffes. With their long necks they leaned toward the red earth, rose to look about, and bent to feed again. Sea gulls, off their course, stopped to perch on the split-rail fences.

The truck stopped in front of a white shack, its paint slightly peeling. A tall man in overalls and a farmer's straw hat appeared around the corner of the house.

"Well, sir," said the man, "here are the little girls to go riding. Hi, there, I'm Sam Anderson." He extended a gnarled, dusty hand.

"And this is our friend, Jane Miller, Sam," said Mr. Garland. "She's never ridden before, so you'll keep good care."

"You bet, Mr. G. By the way, your office called."

As Mr. Garland walked into the house Sam Anderson led the girls around to the barn in back. He hoisted Jane onto a brown-and-white horse and said, "This is called a roan, honey . . . now, is it true that you're from the North? I don't want to tell you anything that you already know."

"Yes, sir, I'm from Chicago," said Jane. "Tell me anything you want to."

Mr. Anderson laughed loudly and said, "Well, take these reins . . . just like this. . . . That's right. Victory, here, will go when you release the reins a little. And when you want to stop, pull back . . . very gently but not *too* gently or she'll take right over. You're the boss now, remember that. She's a good cow pony but a mite tough-mouthed. Keep your knees tight against her sides. And if the goin' gets rough, hold on to this saddle horn."

"This thing?" asked Jane.

"Yep, that thing. After you learn to ride real well we won't let you grab it anymore. Only dudes do that. But for today we'll look the other way . . . right, Sally?"

"Oh, Sam, don't tease her anymore," said Sally.

"Okay, sorry, Jane . . . just kiddin'. Now, let's see you ride around the ring a little."

"Yes, sir," answered Jane. What if I fall off? she thought. What if Victory goes too fast? But she said, "Why is she named Victory?"

"Oh, because Daddy hoped if he named her that, the war might get the idea to end itself sooner," said Sally.

"There's a lot of stuff on the radio today about what the Allies are finding out in Poland and Germany," said Mr. Anderson. "Camps and—"

"Camps for what?" asked Jane. This was the second time she had heard a certain tone in a grown-up's voice. "Camps for what?"

Mr. Anderson looked as if he wanted to take his words back. "Never mind now. It's too good a day to get ourselves all upset. Sally, you ride Jane around the fences and come back in an hour . . . hear? And stay away from the rocks. Those old rattlers will probably come out for a sunbath today."

As the sun grew hotter the smell from Victory's damp

back was that of stables and manure and farm things. The Gulf breeze blew Jane's hair as they rode, and she liked the feel of the cracked leather reins pulling between her fingers.

Mexican workers were bent over in the field as they picked cotton and threw it into large woven baskets. How could they stand for so many hours in the broiling sun? Where did they get water? Who took care of their children?

And then, in a rush, she remembered Mr. Anderson's remarks about the Germans. Would that mean that Jeff would have to go to war sooner? What was happening in those camps?

When they returned to the stables Sam Anderson lifted the saddles from the soaked horses, and the girls walked them around the ring until they had cooled off.

Sally slipped a stiff brush over Jane's hand, a strap crossing the top of her knuckles. "This is a curry comb, Janie. Just brush and brush in one direction until Victory is all smooth again." At first Jane stroked timidly, but soon she was sweeping the comb along Victory's flanks.

When the girls had returned the horses to their stalls and placed feed for them in the door troughs, Sam opened an ancient cooler in the front of the barn and gave them each a bottle of Dr Pepper, so cold Jane had to grasp it with the bottom of her long shirt.

Head tilted back, Jane felt the sweet, fruity liquid trickle into her throat over the icy chunks in the neck of the bottle. Never had she tasted anything so delicious. It was like prunes all mashed up with sugar. The bubbles popped inside her throat and made her eyes water. The chill made her head ache and she shifted her hand on the icy surface. I wonder, she thought, if the mailman came today with Jeff's draft notice.

Chapter 10

"**D**addy, do you think that just once we could have a very small Christmas tree?"

"What did you say?" asked Mr. Miller as he looked up from his book.

"I said, do you think that just once we could have a tiny Christmas tree?"

"Jane, I can't believe you're asking this. It's a very serious question. How do you think the rabbi would answer?"

"He's already been to visit us. He won't come again for a while."

"That's not the point, Jane. We're Jewish. We don't have Christmas trees." Mr. Miller adjusted his glasses and turned a page.

"Daddy, not a big one. Just a little one," said Jane, dropping to the hassock and taking her father's hand. "A really little one with blue-and-white ornaments . . . you know, blue and white like the Jewish flag. It would be a kind of Jewish tree. And the silver tinsel would be silver like our menorah—"

"Grandpa will be here in a few days, Jane. If he saw a tree, he would tear his shirt and you would be dead in his eyes forever." Mr. Miller looked steadily into Jane's eyes. "Would you like that?"

"But Daddy—"

"It's harsh, I know. Grandpa's faith seems old-fashioned. But it gives him great joy. It will give you joy too. Meanwhile, didn't Mother ask you to polish the menorah last week?"

"Yes, but we're out of polish."

"Why didn't you tell her?"

"I forgot."

"Jane!"

"I'm sorry, I'm sorry. I'll do it tomorrow, I promise. And I'll get out the candles."

"Good." Outside, someone turned on a garden hose. The trickling water sounded cool in the hot morning air.

"But I could keep it in my room, and no one would see it. Please? Sally says that Jesus Christ was a Jew, so if that's true, why can't we have a teeny tree to remember him by?"

Mr. Miller closed his book. "Jane, why do you want this tree so badly all of a sudden?"

"Because I saw Sally's. Oh, Daddy, you can't imagine how wonderful it is to decorate it. And it smells of pine needles *all the time,* and the lights sparkle—"

"Listen, Janie . . . come sit by me." She moved into

the big chair. Mr. Miller put his arm around her. "Christmas is not our holiday. It's just not. It belongs to Christians, and if we take their symbol and put it into our house, it's like stealing something sacred."

"But no one would care." Jane bounced up and down on the cushion. "And then we would be like everyone else."

"No, we wouldn't, Jane. We're Jewish. We have Chanukah and it's an important holiday. And it's a beautiful one too. Would you like it if someone . . . let's see . . . if someone took our menorah and used it to light a dinner-party table?"

"It's not the same. The tree is just a pretty thing."

"No, it marks the birth of Christ, Jane. Jesus Christ is not our savior. But Christians believe that when Christ was born, all the trees branched out and flowered in the cold weather."

"Wow!"

"And they believe that the stars on the tree represent the stars that were in heaven that night . . . or something like that."

"Wow!"

"Now, look, you have your own heritage." Mr. Miller placed his cheek next to Jane's. "Chanukah stands for the first time *ever* that people took up arms and fought for their religion. Doesn't that mean a lot to you?"

"Not as much as a Christmas tree."

He sighed. "Our religion can make your life very rich, Janie. Someday you'll understand. Just be patient."

They sat together, each looking in a different direction. The palm tree in the garden whooshed in the wind as the afternoon light crept from the room.

Through the thin walls that night Jane and Jeff heard their parents speaking softly and steadily. Gradually their voices rose. Jane sat up in bed.

"Yes, but he can't have his way all the time, Ruth. Maybe we have to think about this."

"What do you mean, 'think about it'?"

"I'm just saying that for once we should consider ourselves and not be so damned afraid of your father."

"I'm *not* afraid of him. You think of the children all the time anyway. You're always taking their side. You never support me in anything I want to do."

"My God, Ruth, you know I do everything for you that I possibly can—"

"It's *wrong*, Lou."

"Listen, you want to belong to this community. You can't stand not belonging."

"I want to belong to the *Jewish* community. But we can't even do that because we can't *get* there because you can't afford to buy a car."

"All right." Mr. Miller's voice lowered to almost a whisper. "I'll make a deal with you. I'll manage to get a second-hand car if you'll agree to stop complaining and making us all so miserable."

"Who says I make everyone miserable?"

"I do! That boy is going off to war any day. Did you know he registered for the draft yesterday?"

"*No!* Why didn't you tell me?"

"Because you are so unapproachable. You're concerned with no one but yourself. He knew you'd make a terrible scene."

"That's not true."

"It is true. Why do you think he came to me? I went with him to register yesterday. Not you. And I'm telling you Jane is going to have this tree. Let her have *something*! Let her belong *somewhere*! She needs this—and I'll find a car."

"Oh, I just bet you will. Are you going to steal money for that too?"

Mr. Miller's fist hit the wall. Jane ducked under Jeff's arm and hid her face against his chest.

"I'm sorry, Lou . . . I'm sorry. I didn't mean to say that."

"Oh, my God, Ruth."

"I'm sorry. Really." Mrs. Miller was crying now—soft, hiccuping sobs. "Let her have the tree. Let her have it. I do think it's wrong, but one of us should belong somewhere. Let her have it."

"You know I want to do my best, Ruth. You must know that."

"Forget the car. I don't care anymore. Let her have the tree, and I'll find a way to keep it from Papa. One tree, one year—it can't do that much harm. . . ."

A drawer was opened and closed. Jane knew that her mother, staring into the wobbly mirror, would be massaging Pond's cold cream into her face. She heard her father's shoes drop heavily onto the closet floor. Silence.

Jeff tucked Jane into her bed and smoothed back her hair. He made a neat cuff of the white sheet and folded it down over the light blanket. Slipping into his own bed, he pulled up the covers and stared silently at the ceiling. Huge tears slid down his cheeks onto his cotton pajamas. He did not even try to wipe them away.

Chapter 11

J eff had made five dollars mowing lawns, so he
invited Jane to go downtown to the movies the
next Saturday night.

When they emerged from the mildewy theater, the
streets were dark and deserted. They walked to the ice
cream store. Jane had chocolate and Jeff had butterscotch
with bits of praline in it. They sat on the curb in the
flickering light of the neon sign to wait for the bus.

"Why does everyone make such a fuss about Errol
Flynn, Jeff? Even Mom likes him, but I think he's kind of
boring."

"Oh, I don't know. Everyone says he looks so good in
that uniform," Jeff answered, leaning forward to keep the
ice cream from dripping. "I think he's a pretty good ac-
tor, don't you?"

"I don't know," said Jane. "Maybe. But his face is too
thin. Don't you think his face is thin?"

"That's not thin, Jane. That's handsome."

"Then I definitely don't like that kind of handsome." Jane turned her cone and licked the ice cream so that it would be even all around. "I like Sonja Henie's face because it's round and cheery. I like to watch her skate. Maybe if Errol Flynn skated, I wouldn't mind his face so much."

"Maybe," said Jeff.

"Do you think we should have gone to the other movie?" asked Jane.

"Didn't you like this one at all?" Jeff sounded hurt.

"Yes, I did . . . oh, yes, really I did." Jane wanted to pull back the words. "And thank you for taking me, Jeff . . . really. It's just that the movie scared me."

"Why did it scare you?"

"Because there was all that bombing and everything. And people were getting . . . ah . . . uh—"

"Killed? Is that what you mean, Jane?"

"Yes," said Jane, concentrating now on biting the cone so that there would be ice cream left in the little pointed end, the last bit to pop into her mouth.

"So . . . what do you mean? What, Jane?"

"I'm afraid. I'm afraid that . . . oh, never mind."

"You're afraid that maybe I'll be . . . killed, is that it?"

"Don't say that."

"But isn't that what you mean?"

"Yes."

"So am I, Janie." Jeff put his arm around her shoulders.

"But that's what I mean. You'll be drafted. You'll have

to go over there, to Germany, and then you'll be in danger—"

"They won't draft me until after I finish high school."

"But that's this year, Jeff. And you told Mommy and Daddy that you might enlist."

"That was just to make Daddy feel better, Jane—you know, about my not going to Harvard. But sometimes I really believe I should enlist. We're in an awful war and—"

"I don't want you to leave me alone here," Jane said. "Why?"

"You know why . . . because I'm scared of Mommy."

"I know." There was a long pause. "But Jane, sooner or later I've got to go. Do you understand about Hitler and Japan and all that?"

"How can I understand when none of you will explain it to me?"

"It's only because we don't want to scare you. It's just such a terrible time . . . this incredible madman is out there invading countries and wrecking people's lives."

"But wouldn't you be scared to fight, Jeff?"

"Are you crazy? Of course I'm scared, but it will be better than staying around here and studying Texas history and woodworking."

"You hate Corpus Christi, don't you?"

"I do. I just hate it. And I can't stand being around Mom when she cries like that all the time."

"Oh, me too," said Jane as she leaned her head against Jeff's cheek. "And then Daddy yells at her and she screams at him. And his eyes get all red and bloodshot."

"When they do that I know I'll never forget it, not if I

live to be a hundred and ten," Jeff said, looking up at the black sky.

"When I grow up I'm never going to fight with my husband," said Jane. "Anyway, not in front of my children."

"I just don't think I'll ever get married," said Jeff.

"Do you think that other parents hate each other so much?" Jane looked down at her sneakers.

"I think Daddy loves Mom, Jane, but she blames him for failing in business and bringing us here." He paused. "He tries his best. And he's tired."

"I know and it makes me feel so sad. Sometimes he looks as if he doesn't even want to talk anymore." She paused. "Jeff?"

"What?"

"Do you think they'll get a divorce?"

"My God, Jane, what a question! Who have we ever known who got a divorce?"

"Barbara Cooper's parents did. All the kids treated her really badly afterward."

"I remember. No one would talk to her."

"What if Daddy and Mommy got a divorce? How could we stand it?"

"They're not going to get divorced, Jane. Nobody really does that unless—"

"Unless what? Unless they just *hate* each other . . . right?"

"I guess so. But somewhere, way back when, Mom and Dad must have been happier."

"Then why is it so bad now, Jeff?"

"This is hard on Mom. She never had to do any of

these things before, like ironing and washing. She's alone all day while we're at school. And she had to leave her family behind."

"I guess it's lonely for her."

"It must be, Janie. And how do you think she feels when she can't give us a proper dinner?"

"But we're eating much better now."

"Sometimes. But remember when we had suppers of cornflakes and milk when we first got here? If I enlisted, I could—"

"*No,* Jeff!"

"Listen to me, Jane. If I did enlist, I could send some money home."

"Could I go with you after the war, Jeff? I'll be older. We could take care of each other. We could live in a house that's really ours, with a backyard and my pillows from Grandma—"

"Janie, you'll grow up and have your own life. Terrific things will happen for you. When I come out, I could live in Chicago maybe, with all my friends."

"But couldn't I come and visit?"

"Of course. All the time."

"Are you really that homesick?" asked Jane. She took his hand.

"Oh, God, oh, God, yes!" Jeff's eyes clouded over. "I miss Kenny and I miss our cousins and I miss Hyde Park High—sometimes I think I'm going to cry right in class."

"I know, Jeff . . . me too."

"I'll never make it here, Janie. I'm a Yankee. That's how they all think of me, and I can't change. I don't *want* to change. I hate being on the outside though. These kids don't understand me and I don't get them either."

"I feel the same way," said Jane, "but things are beginning to be a little better."

"Oh, that's good, honey."

"But *please* don't go and leave me here. Wait until I can go with you."

"Janie, you just said things were improving for you," Jeff said, rubbing at his scalp.

"But I miss Chicago too. Maybe we'll never go to the Purim party at Aunt Stella's house ever again."

"What do you mean? Do you think you'll never be in Chicago again?"

"Never again probably. Never again in my whole life."

"Of course you will. Why do you think that?"

"Because we don't have the money to go."

"Oh, but we will someday, Jane. You know Daddy will earn more soon. We'll get to go back and visit. It won't be quite the same though."

"What do you mean?"

"It'll be different. Things change all the time."

"Maybe, but if we have a seder here, it will never be the same without Grandpa."

"Yeah, Grandpa does the best seders." He stood up and wiped his hands with the soggy paper napkins. "Wouldn't it be swell to go to a real museum again?"

"Oh, yes," said Jane, "the Art Institute, especially. We could see all the miniature rooms and that girl that Sargent drew, you know, she's looking over her shoulder.

And those people in the park in France . . . what's that called?"

" 'Sunday Afternoon on the Isle of—"

"—the Grande Jatte.' By Georges Seurat, I remember now. The parasols and the baby buggy and the old lady under the tree."

"And we could see Uncle Burt and Uncle Mel," added Jeff, "even if they're not speaking to Daddy."

"And Grandpa would build the sukkah in October," said Jane.

"And climb up too high, like a screwball, to hang the grapes." Jeff smiled at the memory of Grandpa on the little latticed hut.

"And everyone would yell, Grandpa, come down from there this minute—you're going to kill yourself," said Jane.

Jeff sat down abruptly and covered his face with his hands. "Oh, Jane, I want to go home . . . I want to go home." Jane threw her arms around him as he wept. And then she, too, cried, burying her face in his neck.

Finally they grew calmer. Jeff took a handkerchief from his pocket, and holding Jane's face by the chin, he wiped her tears.

They sat, elbows on knees, staring into the street. Jeff smoothed away a bit of ice cream that had fallen on Jane's pedal pushers.

"Thank you," she said. The moon rose higher over the low, wooden buildings, and they waited for the bus.

Chapter 12

"Come on, Jane. Get your straw hat. The sun's very bad." Mr. Miller waved a set of keys in the air.

"Where are we going? Whose keys are those?"

"It's a surprise. Come on. I've borrowed a car."

"Louis, she can't go," called Mrs. Miller from the kitchen. "She's got a lot of work to do here."

"Now, dear," said Mr. Miller as he stood in the kitchen doorway, "let her off for an hour or two. She'll help you when she gets back, won't you, Janie?"

"Papa's coming, you know that, Louis. I can't run this house all by myself." Mrs. Miller was stirring broth that sent chicken-scented mists into the air and partly obscured her face.

"Ruth, let her go. You should come too." Mr. Miller tucked an escaping strand of hair behind his wife's ear.

"Dad, may I go?" Jeff entered the kitchen.

"Yes, but it's a surprise, so don't ask too many questions, all right? Get your hat."

"But Louis, I don't want to be left with all these things to do—"

"Ruth, these kids have worked all morning. Your father doesn't get here for days. They're coming with me. Take a ride with us."

"No, thank you. *Someone* has to get everything ready. There's no maid here, you know."

"Oh, for God's sake, Ruth—"

"All right, Mom, I'll stay," said Jeff, "but let Jane go— so at least Daddy doesn't have to drive alone."

"Enough is enough!" Mr. Miller's eyes widened and the fierce red veins appeared in them. His forehead grew glossy with sweat and he shouted, "Ruth, you are doing this—"

"Never mind, never mind," she said, turning back to the stove. "But just remember that when you come back, there are a lot of things to do. Go on, all of you—I don't want to discuss it anymore."

Mr. Miller had borrowed a blue Studebaker convertible. No wonder he wanted us to bring hats, thought Jane happily as she sat down inch by inch on the hot beige leather seat.

Jeff sat in front and ran his hand over the gnarled wooden dashboard. "What a car! Where did you get this? Look at these dials and the clock . . . and there's a fantastic radio too."

"It belongs to a friend from the temple," said Mr. Miller.

Christmas decorations were everywhere along Ocean

Drive. Wreaths tied with glistening red bows hung on massive doors, and Christmas trees pressed against closed windows. Bushes and shrubs draped with fake candy canes and ornaments drooped in the heat. On the roof of a pink adobe mansion an enormous spangled star sent shots of light toward the car as it passed.

At one house a Mexican maid approached a tennis court where four people, all in white, were laughing, bent double over something so hilarious that they couldn't play.

In Chicago Jane's father had played tennis with Uncle Burt and Jeff every Saturday. Sometimes the fourth person couldn't come, so Uncle Burt—his long legs sticking out of her mother's little telephone closet in the hall—had to dial number after number to find someone else to play.

Mr. Miller would swing his racket in an imaginary serve, his white shorts and knee-high socks glowing in the dim hallway.

"It's *'yes,'*" Uncle Burt would call out. "Joel will play. Bye, little girl. Come on, Jeff." Then Uncle Burt would lift Jane into the air and kiss her cheeks, the rough material of his shirt scratching against her face.

Jane would stand at the leaded windows and watch them pile into the car. An hour or so later Mrs. Miller would leave to play golf. Her starched shirt and skirt crackled as she gathered up her golf bag and placed it on her shoulder. She would draw Jane in with her free arm and say, "Good-bye, Janie. Have a good time at ballet school, and we'll see you tonight."

Where were those parents now? And the old Jeff?

Today, however, as they drove, Mr. Miller looked

peaceful. The wind ruffled his short gray hair and blew his tie into a patterned flag.

It was Sunday and empty streets stretched in all directions. Only the Nueces Hotel sign still flickered, its neon light turning the sidewalk below first red and then blue and then red again.

They came to a neighborhood of shanties and one-room cabins. People were putting up crèches in their yards. Jane loved to see the baby Jesus in his crib of straw. She always wanted to crawl into the crèche—it was like a big doll's house—and become a part of the scene.

Mr. Miller stopped at the train depot.

"Is Grandpa coming today? Is that the surprise?" asked Jeff.

A train lumbered into view. A boxcar door opened, and a man began throwing bundles and boxes to the stationmaster, who had rolled a dolly to the edge of the track.

"I got a box here marked Fragile," said the man, "from a bakery in San Antonio."

"Excuse me," said Mr. Miller, approaching the boxcar, "that may be for me. Is it addressed to Miller?"

"Yes."

"Well, here I am," said Mr. Miller, wiping his forehead with a handkerchief. "Would you like to see the receipt?"

"No, not necessary," said the stationmaster. "Glad to get it delivered. Here you go. God, that's heavy!"

Jeff threw his arms open wide. "Dad, aren't you going to tell us what's in there?"

"They're . . . bagels," Mr. Miller said.

The railroad men looked at each other. They didn't

know what a bagel was! The word suddenly felt foreign to Jane too.

Jane and Jeff jumped up and down and reached for the box. They hugged it and thumped it loudly.

"You found bagels in *Texas,* Daddy?"

"How did you do it?"

"Get in the car, children, and I'll explain. Thank you for your trouble, gentlemen, and Merry Christmas to you."

"And a merry one to you too," said the trainmaster.

"Where did you get them?" Jane leaned over, her head resting on the seat between Jeff and her father.

"Someone told me about a bakery in San Antonio where they send out special orders."

"But Daddy, Grandpa will be here and he won't eat them. They're not kosher."

"Yes, they are, Jane. I have a certificate to show Grandpa. He won't be able to challenge me on this one."

"Boy, Dad," Jeff said, "you've thought of everything. Did they cost a lot?"

"Well, son, enough so that we get to order them only this once. Perhaps one day we'll be able to find some lox and decent cream cheese down here. Wouldn't that be something?"

"Oh, yes . . . *great,* Daddy." As they drove home Jane held up her hands, just like Jeff, to catch the fragrant Gulf air blowing hotly into the car.

Chapter 13

Surrounded by piles of silver tinsel, Jeff and Jane sat on the edge of Jeff's bed and looked at the tiny tree. The little branches were so small that Jane cut the shiny strands in half with a pair of scissors.

"Mrs. Garland gave me a taste of eggnog. It's really creamy and it has nutmeg on top. It was so good."

"Don't tell Mom."

"Are Jewish people allowed to drink eggnog?"

"God only knows. Better not tell Grandpa either, come to think of it."

"And you know that day I rode horses with Sally?"

"Yes."

"Well, after we combed the horses—with something called a *curry comb* . . . do you know about that?"

"No, Janie," replied Jeff as he pressed out some tinsel with the palm of his hand.

"We drank some Dr Peppers afterward that were so cold you could see long sticks of ice in them."

"Sounds great to me."

"Jeff?"

"Now what?"

"Do you think that Jews are allowed to drink Dr Pepper?"

"Some Orthodox Jews wouldn't—unless it was blessed by a rabbi. And it's probably not . . . I mean, is there a kosher bottling plant in Houston or Beaumont or somewhere?"

"Do you think there might be one of those rabbis in Texas—you know, the ones who bless food?"

"For God's sake, Jane, I don't know."

"Oh, well," said Jane, "I hope I didn't do anything wrong."

"Of course you didn't. We don't keep kosher. Grandpa does, but we don't have to worry about obeying all those rules. Why are you so worried?"

"I don't know. He cares so much about all that stuff . . . about being Jewish. I hate it when he starts waving his arms around and preaching. I know he loves us, but—"

"Yeah, he can make things so hard, but then there's that funny light around him sometimes when he's praying or talking about being a Jew. It actually shines! I swear it does! Then I kind of understand him."

"You're right! But Jeff, don't you feel like shouting Leave us alone . . . I mean, to just let us be whatever kind of Jews we are?"

"Sure, but he's the only person I know who *cares* so much about something. I wish I cared about something that much."

"Don't you?"

"Only about getting away."

"Don't start that again!"

"Okay, Janie. But you know how I feel. It's going to happen sooner or later."

For a while they worked in silence, accompanied by music coming from one of the other cabins: "I'm dreaming of a white Christmas . . ." From the highway came the rumbling of the navy trucks carrying sailors, singing off-key Christmas carols: "Thu-u-UH fir-r-rst No-o-o-EL-L-L the-e-e angels did say-y-y-y . . ."

"Jeff?"

"What?"

"What if I wore real cowboy boots? Do you think Jews—"

"Jane!"

"But do you think God would mind?"

"For pete's sake, Jane, God doesn't know anything about cowboy boots."

"Okay, okay, just asking."

"Look, I don't mean to shout at you . . . but I don't think God cares what we wear. I mean, we're at war now. Jews are wearing helmets and boots, for sure—combat boots—do you think it matters to Him? And we're wearing battle fatigues and navy-blues and camouflage clothes. It doesn't matter what you look like—"

"It matters what you do," added Jane.

"Right," said Jeff, mussing her hair.

"Well, that's my whole point," said Jane. "I don't always know what to do."

"Neither does anyone else, Janie."

"What do you mean?"

"Well, I'm going to be wearing a uniform pretty soon. And I'll have to carry a gun or fly a plane and drop bombs —maybe kill somebody. I don't think people should do that."

"But I heard you say this is a 'good war.' "

"It is—I mean, I think it is. But I hate the idea of carrying a weapon."

"David had a weapon. He killed Goliath," offered Jane.

"Yeah, but that was just a slingshot, and I don't think he felt so great about doing that."

"Then why do the pictures in books always show him standing up straight and looking so proud?"

"Good point. I don't know."

They stood back to look at their handiwork. The tree shimmered in the sunlight. Jane opened a cardboard box with six compartments inside. They put hooks in each blue star. A few strands of tinsel clung to the bedspreads. Pine needles mixed with grains of sand from the beach scratched their knees as they moved about on the floor. Finally Jeff turned on a switch. Five blue lights glowed from deep within the tree.

"Oohhhhh." Jane sighed as she put her arms around Jeff's waist. "It's so beautiful."

"There you are, Janie. There's your tree."

"It's not really a tree. It's more like a . . . a . . . Chanukah bush."

"Try telling that to Grandpa," said Jeff.

Chapter 14

T he smell of harsh soap and disinfectant per-
meated the small kitchen. Mrs. Miller was
scrubbing out a cupboard. Piles of china and
silverware lay on the floor, and in the corners of the room
were cardboard boxes with half-open lids.

Mr. Miller, his hands covered with suds and bits of
steel wool, scoured the top burners of the stove. Jane sat
on the floor, wrapping silverware in soft cloths.

"Mrs. Miller, excuse me, but you didn't hear me
knock." Sally, barefoot, in her bathing suit, stood in the
doorway.

"Well, Sally, nice to see you," said Mr. Miller. "Come
in and have some lemonade."

"Oh, Lou, I look such a mess," said Mrs. Miller.

"Oh, Mom, we all look terrible," said Jane, hoping
Sally would not go away. Why did Mother say things like
that?

"Indeed we do. Come on, Sally, have some lemon-ade," said Mr. Miller.

"No, thanks, Mr. Miller—I just had lunch, but I'll help ya'll . . . whatever it is ya'll are doin'.'"

"How thoughtful of you, Sally," said Mrs. Miller. "Would you like to help Jane wrap up the silver?"

"Sure. Are ya'll gettin' ready to paint or somethin'?"

"No, Sally," said Mr. Miller. "Mrs. Miller's father is coming, and we are changing over the kitchen for him."

"We're making the kitchen kosher," said Mrs. Miller.

"What does *kosher* mean?" asked Sally.

"Fit or *proper,"* said Mr. Miller as he scoured the oven racks.

"Fit or proper for what?" asked Jane. "I never knew what exactly that meant, Daddy."

"Well, let's see . . . fit or proper for—"

"Eating . . . eating," said Mrs. Miller, casting an impatient look at her husband.

"But I've eaten here," said Sally. "Everything is very fit and proper, and very clean. Doesn't your father like your food, Mrs. Miller?"

"No, he doesn't, as a matter of fact," said Mr. Miller. "We mix our dairy products with meat, and Orthodox Jews won't eat from plates that have had that mixture on them, so you see—"

"Oh, so you get new plates and things for him, is that it?" asked Sally.

"Well, we have to get two new sets of everything," said Mrs. Miller. "We just put our set away when Papa comes to visit. Also, Sally, Orthodox Jews will eat only animals that have been killed a certain way, so—"

"Ugh! What way?"

"Oh, yes, Mom, *ugh!*" Jane joined Sally in making a face. "*What* way?"

"It's fairly complicated, girls," said Mr. Miller as he attacked another oven rack. "It all comes from Jewish law, from the Book of Deuteronomy."

"And you have to do this every time he comes to visit?" asked Sally.

"Yes," said Mrs. Miller, removing newspaper from glass plates in the large boxes, "and it's a lot of work and a lot of trouble."

"But you do it *every time*? Even if he comes twice a year . . . or more?"

"Well, Sally, he's my father," replied Mrs. Miller. "I have to. Anyway, I've always done it, so I shouldn't complain."

"I hope you remember what you just said," muttered Mr. Miller.

"I don't remember making such a fuss over the years," snapped Mrs. Miller.

"Are you listening to yourself?" asked her husband.

"Louis, I just hate it when you *lie about me!*" Mrs. Miller's voice was rising to a shriek. "And Jane is not going to play while I *work.*"

Jane saw Sally's amazed look. "Mother, what else can we do?"

"*Nothing,* Jane! If you don't *know* what has to be done, then I'm not going to tell you."

"Ruth, let the girls go now. They've been a great help. Didn't you want to wash that shell collection you found this morning, Jane?" asked Mr. Miller.

"Yes, Daddy, thank you."

"Louis!" Mrs. Miller sputtered. "There are so many things to do! How can you let her go?"

"Ruth, I'm here. I'll help you."

Sally, shifting from foot to foot, said, "Well, thank you for letting me stay . . . I learned a lot."

"Thank you for helping, Sally," said Mrs. Miller, lowering her voice.

"Stay for a while and play with Jane," said Mr. Miller. Mrs. Miller sighed and turned away.

"Thank you, I will," said Sally.

They sat in the old metal chairs on the lawn and carefully washed the shells, which Jane had left in a bucket by the palm tree. One by one, they were placed on the scrappy grass to dry.

"These are really excellent," said Sally. "Where did you find them?"

"I went down the beach toward the naval base, but don't tell Mom. I've never gone that far before, and she'd be furious."

"I won't." Sally smiled and they exchanged a look. Sally had seen how fearsome Jane's mother could be, but she was not going to say anything. Jane was grateful for Sally's sensitive good manners.

"These shells were in a little inlet . . . you know, a secret cove."

"Wow, Jane! Will you take me there?" Putting her hand on Jane's shoulder, Sally gave a little squeeze.

Jane's eyes began to water. "Oh, sure. But first you have to come and see what I have in my room."

Jane closed the door of her room, pulled down the

water-stained shades, opened the closet, and pulled out the tiny tree. As she plugged in the lights Sally clapped her hands. "That is the cutest thing I ever did see! Where on earth did you get it?"

"My father bought it for me," said Jane, adjusting one of the blue glass stars.

"But I thought you told me you never had a tree—that Jews weren't supposed to have them."

"I never did have one. They just let me do this for the first time."

"But why?"

"I really don't know, Sally," said Jane. "At least . . . not for sure, I don't."

"But your grandfather's coming. He won't like it, will he?"

"He'll kill me if he finds it. But he won't because we'll keep it hidden in here most of the time."

"But aren't you afraid?"

"Yes, I am, but I've got to do it."

Sally dropped to her knees. "Oh, it's the sweetest little thing, Jane. But you know, you really need more on it. You don't mind my sayin' that, do you?"

"No, but Daddy said that was really all we should spend," Jane replied. She didn't want to remember how her father had painfully counted out pennies and nickels to pay for the tinsel and hooks. And how upset he was when he realized that a metal stand was needed, and he had to rummage in his pockets to find his last dollar to give the man in the parking lot where the trees were sold.

"Do you want some more stuff, Jane? We could make

some cranberry strings and folded paper birds and pop-corn chains . . . things like that—"

"I don't know how to make them."

"Come to my house, silly. I'll show you how. We've got popcorn and everything . . . berries and paper and crayons, you know. Jo will fix us soft custard with cinna-mon. Want to?"

"If my mother says I can."

Sally looked at Jane. "If your mother says no, my mother will call her."

"No, no . . . I'm sure it will be all right. Tonight, you mean?"

"Yes. Can you?"

"I will. I mean I'll really try. Thank you."

"Good deal!" And Sally, giving Jane a quick hug, ran across the gravel path, the oleander bushes parting like a red curtain and popping back as she disappeared from sight.

Chapter 15

That night Sally and Jane sat on the sun-room floor, the Garlands' gigantic tree glowing behind them. Sally showed Jane how to cut construction paper into birds, and they made paper chains with fringed edges. There were bowls of cranberries and popcorn ready to string. Josephine had brought in two red mugs of steaming vanilla custard and a cinnamon shaker. "Now, listen, young ladies, not a drop of anythin' on these good rugs, hear me?"

"See, Jane, you hold this paper while I glue it, and then you wave it in the air until it dries."

"What is this?"

"It's the wing of one of the birds. Now we'll attach it to the body."

"But how do we hang the birds on the tree?"

"We'll get my daddy's hole puncher, and then we'll put those little paper hooks through the holes. I can't believe you don't know how to do this. Didn't you do it in your school in Chicago?"

"No," said Jane, running around the room: *"Vro-o-o-o-om, vro-o-o-o-om, whish, whis-s-s-s-sh,"* she cried as the striped paper bird wheeled and dipped and soared in her hand.

"Jane, why don't Jews have trees?"

"It's not our holiday, you know. We don't believe in Jesus Christ." She ran with the bird. *"Vro-o-o-o-om, vro-o-o-o-om, whish . . ."*

"You told me that before," said Sally, folding a circle of paper over her finger and dabbing it with white paste. "I just can't get over it."

"Inez Richardson said I will go to hell because I'm not a Christian." Jane stopped. "I almost slugged her."

Sally looked up. "She said that to your face?"

"She said that Janice Burke's brother said so when he preached in that big tent last week."

"Howard Burke said that?"

"That's what Inez told me."

"He said *you* would go to hell, Jane?"

"Yes, but he meant all Jews, I guess, because we don't believe that Jesus died for us."

Sally stapled a circle of paper atop the bird's head. "Why don't you think Jesus died for you?"

"I'm not exactly sure," said Jane, bringing the paper bird in for a landing beneath the tree. "Grandpa says we're still waiting for our messiah. Jesus just wasn't the one."

"Who will be the one?"

"Grandpa says we'll know it when he gets here."

"When is that supposed to be?"

"Anytime now, I guess."

"But Jane, do you think you might really go to hell? Howard's not in our church, so I'm never sure what he's talkin' about."

"No!" Jane took another sip of her custard. "My grandpa says that heaven and hell are right here on this earth. He says that we make our own heaven and hell by what we do when we're living our lives. Here, this bird is really dry now."

"Thanks. This is really a good one. But why do you think Janice's brother said that, Janie? Was he just trying to scare you?"

"What about Janice's brother? Howard, you mean?" Mrs. Garland had entered the room in a long plaid skirt and white satin shirt. "Why was he tryin' to scare Jane?"

"Oh," said Jane, gazing at the graceful, swinging motion of the pearls under Mrs. Garland's collar. She looked like one of those models on the cover of a magazine in the dentist's office.

"Now, come on, Sally . . . what about Howard?"

"Mama, he said that all Jews will go to hell because they don't believe that Jesus Christ is their savior."

"Oh, that boy is impossible," exclaimed Mrs. Garland, biting down on the cigarette holder. Little puffs of smoke darted into the air. "What does he know about Jews or anythin' else? Born with a silver spoon chokin' him to death, never traveled farther than Amarillo. How dare he say such a thing!"

"Yes, ma'am," replied Sally.

"Jane, where did you hear that?" asked Mrs. Garland.

"Inez Richardson told her, Mama."

"Oh, for God's sake . . . these kids with foolish mouths! Listen, Jane dear, pay no mind to stupid people. We have to let everyone in the world have a go-round with God in his own way."

"Yes, ma'am," said Jane.

"Things won't be easy for you. They're not easy for anyone who seems to be different. Just be brave."

"Yes, ma'am."

"You have to stand up for what you believe. You know perfectly well you're not going to hell—if there is such a place—don't you?"

"Yes, ma'am, but it made me feel odd when Inez told me that."

"Well, of course it did. Ignore her. Ignore that silly Howard Burke. I am going to call his mother right now and shout at her. How dare he! Sandra Burke has spoiled that boy to death, and now he's going around judgin' people. He should get out of this state and hear some ideas that would broaden his narrow little mind. What are you doin', girls?"

Jane jumped at the abrupt change of subject. You never knew what Mrs. Garland was going to do! "We're making some ornaments for Jane's tree, Mama."

"You have a tree, Jane? Good heavens, how did that happen?"

"I don't know, Mrs. Garland," said Jane, feeling red heat creep over her face. "My parents said I could do it, this once."

"Well, there you go—you see, we all should try everythin'. Are you having fun with it?"

"Yes, ma'am, I am."

"Good, dear. Enjoy it and embrace it. I'm callin' Sandra Burke now to yell until the fig trees bloom. Do you girls want more custard?"

"Yes, Mama, that would be nice," said Sally.

"I'll stick my head into the kitchen on the way to the phone. Have fun, cuties." And with a wave of the cigarette holder, she strode out of the room, her skirt kicking up bits of paper and tinsel and her mousy brown hair puffing up behind her as if it were a crown.

Chapter 16

T he next day Jane put all the new ornaments on her tree. From her window she could see Mrs. Miller in a beltless housedress, a bandanna folded around her hair, trimming the rose bush in the side yard. Jeff was wheeling his bicycle from the garage.

There was a slow crunching of gravel as a large maroon Buick moved up the narrow path and stopped. An impossibly tall man in a camel-color suit and a new Stetson unfolded himself out of the car. He turned and opened the back door, and two enormous, dusty, black, high-top shoes, followed by two endless trousered legs, planted themselves upon the ground.

A lean, noble head with a yarmulke perched firmly on neatly trimmed white hair bent low and then slowly upward, pulling behind it a six-foot body in clothes that had once been black, but now had a worn, brownish-purple sheen.

Grandpa! Two days early? Why hadn't he telephoned? Jane twirled from the window and looked at the little tree. Her heart pounding, she dropped to her knees and tried to move it back into the closet.

But the tree was caught somehow and refused to budge.

Mrs. Miller, shears in hand, bolted past Jane's window. "Papa, what are you doing here so soon? We didn't expect you for two more days."

"I left Chicago early, so that I could be here for the first night of Chanukah. You haven't changed over the dishes?"

"No, Papa, I have, I have. It's just that I'm surprised, that's all."

"This gentleman is Doggie McCabe. He gave me a ride from San Antonio when the train broke down. This is my daughter, Ruth Miller, and this is my grandson, Jeff."

The ornaments on the tree swayed crazily as Jane tried to move it. Tinsel waved and dry needles fell. A blue star crashed to the floor. If she lifted up the tree, everything would fall off. Jane glanced out the window. Her mother and Jeff were looking anxiously toward the house. She dropped back to the floor.

"Jane! Jane! Grandpa's here." Jeff ran into the bedroom with Grandpa's bags. "For God's sake, put the tree away."

"Can't you see what I'm doing?" She dashed around the room. *Help me!*"

Jeff nearly threw the bags down in the doorway.

"You've got the plug in." He pulled it out of the wall so hard that it swung into the branches, tearing loose some cranberries, popcorn, and two of the glass decorations.

They dove in two directions after the ornaments and stuffed them into their pockets. As he squeezed under the dresser, Jeff's foot crunched a blue glass star into a thousand sharp pieces.

"You idiot!" whispered Jane hoarsely as she reached beneath the bed for a paper chain. "How are we ever going to sweep that up?"

"We can't now," cried Jeff. "Get that little rug and throw it over the whole mess. Then I'll push the tree back."

"What if he comes in?" asked Jane, arranging the braided rug over the shards.

"He won't! Mom's going to keep him talking out there." Jeff scooped up some cranberries and shoved them into his socks. He lifted the tree a few inches and settled it in the closet, behind Jane's clothes, and closed the door.

There was a last frantic rush as they smoothed the bedspreads, picked up straying bits of tinsel and pine needles, and put them under the rug.

"Jane, go out there so Grandpa won't think anything is wrong. I'll put his bags in his room and take care of the rest."

"Oh, thanks, thanks, Jeff." She almost cried from fear and relief.

"Hurry!" he rasped, and pushed her toward the living room.

"Grandpa, you're here," cried Jane, racing across the tiny lawn.

"Where have you been?" He opened his arms wide. "Mr. McCabe, this is my very own granddaughter, Jane. Janie, meet Doggie McCabe, who just saved my life."

"How do you do," said Jane as she was buried in the jacket of the wrinkled, almost black suit.

"How do you do, Jane," answered Mr. McCabe. "Your grandfather kept me real good company on the ride down."

"And how about a kiss from you, little girl?" asked Grandpa.

This, Jane knew, was her cue. "Oh, Grandpa," she said, regaining her breath. Glancing quickly toward the house, she put her hands on his hips like an actress in an old-fashioned Western movie. She posed for a moment and then said, "Oh dear, oh dear, your mustache is so scratchy. Do I have to kiss you?"

"Yes, you do," answered Grandpa, projecting his lines with great relish. "Because you know what the Torah says."

"What does the Torah say?" asked Jane.

"The Torah says that a kiss without a mustache—"

"—is like an egg without salt!" finished Jane as she was enfolded once more into his sharp, bony embrace.

Everyone laughed. "Have a pleasant stay, Mr. Brodin. Good-bye, ladies." Mr. McCabe bowed and slipped into the front seat of the car.

"Oh, Mr. Brodin, I almost forgot. Here's your food." He handed Grandpa two rumpled paper bags. Jane knew that inside would be hard-boiled eggs, cans of fish, and oranges. Kosher food. Or whatever was left of it.

"Thank you for everything," Grandpa said, taking the bags.

"Welcome. You're welcome." The big Buick rolled up the path to Ocean Drive, and everyone waved.

Jeff came running out of the house. Mrs. Miller raised her eyebrows and glanced quickly from Jeff to Jane.

"Papa, you must be very tired," she said, leading her father toward the house.

"Well, a bath would be a very nice thing," answered Grandpa. "Where's Louis—working?"

"He is, Papa," said Mrs. Miller, bending over slightly and patting her chest in short little beats, as if searching for more air.

"Well, children, what's been happening? What new things have you to show me?" asked Grandpa.

Jane's mouth formed a frightened O. Jeff turned quickly to look at his grandfather.

"Why is everyone so jumpy around here? If you have Chanukah presents, just hide them. I won't look."

Mrs. Miller had moved ahead and was scanning the children's room. Shutting the door behind her, she walked back to her father and said, "Oh, yes, Papa, lots of presents, but we have hidden them now, so the emergency is over. We do, however, have some nice bagels for you."

"Are they kosher? Where did they come from?"

"Yes, they're kosher. Lou ordered them. An extravagance, but it's only for this once."

"They will taste very good," said Grandpa. "Now, tell me more. Jeff, have you registered for the draft?"

"I did, Grandpa," said Jeff.

"Oh, this war. God bless you, Jeff. God bless us all. Let's just hope we survive, if God wills it. And what about you, Janie? What interesting things are going on around here? New books? Any surprises for your grandfather?"

"Uh, no, Gramps, no . . . I don't think so."

Jeff and Mrs. Miller looked studiously at their hands and feet as Grandpa headed for the little office that would be his room. "And now," he inquired, "who would like to draw a bath for me?"

Chapter 17

Grandpa rested the next day. On Thursday he said, "Jane, I'm taking the bus to Braslau's Furniture Store to sell some ties. Would you like to come? They're expecting me."

On Ocean Drive the breeze blew through the windows of the rickety bus. In the rear seats were Negro maids, going back to town from their jobs. In the middle rows sat Mexican gardeners who held their gunnysacks of tools. Up front, behind Jane and Grandpa, two sailors sang songs and laughed at a joke.

A group of Jewish men had assembled at Braslau's Furniture Store. Jane had met most of these men. Some of them were Orthodox, like Grandpa. They probably didn't really need any of the gaudy ties and belts and packaged handkerchiefs Grandpa had to sell. Were they there because they felt sorry for him? Jane looked at

Grandpa's threadbare suit, the cuffs dangling little strings. She wanted to reach over and pull them off.

"Gentlemen," said Grandpa, "do you know my pride and joy—my little granddaughter, Jane Miller?"

"We surely do," answered Mr. Braslau. "How are your folks, Jane?"

"They're fine, sir."

"And how about you, Jane?" asked one of the other men. "Have you made lots of friends?"

"Yes, sir . . . some."

"And are you here today as your grandfather's assistant?" asked Mr. Goldberg, who owned the drugstore.

"No, sir, I'm just here to keep Grandpa company."

"Well, good," replied Mr. Braslau, "and what have you got for us today, Leon? Any new things since September?"

Grandpa held up a broad tie printed with polka dots and palm trees. "Gentlemen, I picked out this collection just before I came to Corpus Christi. These things are being shown in New York, and in Chicago too. Very up-to-the-minute, as I'm sure you can see."

One of the men turned away his head to smile.

Grandpa, Jane prayed, put the tie down and show a different one.

"Anyone interested in cummerbunds? I have them in red and plaid and black."

Mr. Sheinberg yawned, and Mr. Green, sprawled in one of the chairs, examined his fingernails and sighed.

Jane nearly stamped her foot. She wanted to shake the men and make them pay attention. Why had they agreed to come there if they were going to hurt his feelings?

Grandpa began to hum a little Hebrew melody as he quietly spread out white handkerchiefs and ties on the countertop. He draped his arms with belts and waved them gently like display racks. He hummed a little louder. Mr. Green sat up and craned his neck to see the merchandise.

"Now, there's a belt I like," said Mr. Goldberg as he began to hum along with Grandpa. "What is that tune, Mr. Brodin? My mother sang it."

"It's '*Al Tashlicheinu*'" said Grandpa, doing one of his little dance steps.

"Oh, I remember now," said Mr. Green. "We sang it, too, *da-de-da-da-da-da* . . . Oh, this is a very nice tie, Mr. Brodin. Do you have it in another color?"

"How about this one? Same pattern, different color stripes." Grandpa sang the sentence and all the men laughed. The tight place between Jane's shoulders relaxed a bit. A few of the men moved slowly to the counter and held shirts up to their chests.

"Try this one, Carl. It's got an eastern collar."

"Mr. Brodin, do you have this polo shirt in my size?"

"Yes, indeed. *Da-da-da-dum* . . . How about in blue?"

"Yes, perfect. *Da-da-de-de-da-dum.* Just perfect."

"Looks good, Mr. Danziger. *Da-da-da-dum, dee* . . ."

As Grandpa wrapped up purchases with plain white paper and used twine, Mr. Goldberg and Mr. Pearle, who ran the dry cleaner's, began to copy Grandpa's dance steps.

"Your grandfather can really cut a rug, Jane. Did you teach him?" asked Mr. Stein.

"No," Jane said, "he's the best dancer in our family." It was true. All the cousins loved to be held in Grandpa's arms as he whirled them around. When Jane was very small she had stood with her tiny feet on his big galumpy shoes, and holding Grandpa's hands, she'd pretended that she was really dancing on her own. The lace collar on her black velvet dress would fly up and cover her mouth, and Grandpa's large white teeth would flash below his mustache as he sang and dipped about the room.

"I must say, Mr. Brodin, I didn't know that Orthodox Jews could dance so well," said Mr. Berman.

"Mr. Berman, to be a Jew is a joyous thing. The Talmud encourages us to love life."

"Speaking of that, Mr. Brodin, there's a question I know you could answer for me," said Mr. Braslau, handing Grandpa a tie for him to wrap up.

"What is that, sir?"

"Well, I have a friend in Louisville, a widower, who is going to marry his late wife's sister."

"Yes. Often done, according to Jewish law," said Grandpa, laying out some colored silk handkerchiefs.

"But what if they don't love each other? Is this law a good thing?"

"Mr. Braslau," answered Grandpa as he rewound an alligator belt around his wrist, "they may *think* they don't love each other, but God takes care of them and they join together in His light. Do you love your wife?"

"Well, of course," answered Mr. Braslau. "What a question! Jane, cover your ears."

"And how long have you been married?"

"Thirty-seven years."

"And has it been thirty-seven totally wonderful years?"

"Well, it has been . . . it has been . . ."

"Exactly my point, Mr. Braslau. There have been happy days and not-so-happy days, but you are still together and I'm sure you have a wonderful family life. Nothing is perfect, but God takes care of us all, if you see what I mean."

The men began to chuckle and move closer, like students surrounding their rabbi on Friday night. They wanted to touch him. Mr. Bernstein affectionately patted Grandpa's shoulder. There was a brush of fingers across his arm, a friendly touch of his hand.

"Mr. Brodin, would you like some iced tea?" asked Mr. Braslau.

"No, thank you," answered Grandpa.

Jane knew that he was afraid the kitchen behind the store might not be kosher. Too bad, because she was so thirsty!

The room was now full of gaiety. Mr. Green and Mr. Sheinberg were exchanging snatches of songs, and Mr. Braslau was doing a funny tap dance on a piece of linoleum. Some of the other men were laughing and trying on black cummerbunds and silk bow ties. On the floor was a large pile of the neatly wrapped packages, and as the late afternoon sun spilled across the overstuffed couches and chairs, everyone seemed to have forgotten that there were customers to serve and businesses to run.

Grandpa was growing tired. He jerked his head up

from time to time, as if to keep alert. "Mr. Golden wants to know if they'll see you in *shul* on *Shabbos,* Grandpa," Jane said, stepping in to help him pack his case.

"I've lived seventy-three years and have never missed a Saturday morning, my friends . . . or a Friday night. So I'll surely see you, God willing."

"Good, good," said Mr. Sheinberg, "I'll save you a place."

"And next year I'll return with a new collection, gentlemen, so have your shekels ready."

"We will, Mr. Brodin. We will!"

"And God bless you all."

"And you too, sir . . . you too!"

"Thank you, gentlemen," said Grandpa, rising and holding on to Jane's shoulder. She could feel his hand tremble. "I appreciate your patronage, and the company has been stimulating."

"Our pleasure! Our pleasure! We have enjoyed it," they said as they all stepped forward to shake his hand. Jane and Grandpa were escorted to the door. "What a wonderful grandfather you have, Jane," said Mr. Green.

"Yes, sir, I think so too."

"Good-bye, Mr. Brodin," said Mr. Braslau, shaking Grandpa's hand. "Please tell your children that if they need anything at all for their house, I'll be delighted to give them a discount."

"I will, thank you, sir," said Grandpa, tipping his hat.

Then they were once more on the sizzling sidewalk. Grandpa's display case was sweating in the sun, and he shifted it from hand to hand. Jane was hungry and tired.

Across the street, as they walked slowly toward the bus stop, was the Greek café with its sign swinging in the wind: GULF SHRIMP. ALL YOU CAN EAT.

"*Oy,*" said Grandpa. "*Traife.*"

Chapter 18

On the fourth day of Chanukah it was so hot that big black bubbles of asphalt popped like angry craters on Ocean Drive, and traffic was detoured for miles. Drenched with perspiration, his wet coat held over one shoulder, Mr. Miller trudged up the hill, *The Corpus Christi Caller-Times* held up under one arm. His heavy briefcase pulled his shoulder into a lopsided curve.

Waiting in the sandy yard, Jane noticed that the newsprint had come off on his sleeve and on the side of his face, making him look muddled and gray, as if he had been repairing the damaged road. Her heart lurched. He looks so tired, she thought.

Mrs. Miller had put a fan in the living room, and the thin curtains struggled in its breeze. In the front yards of the tourist court, overturned tricycles had been abandoned by children too hot to ride them anymore. Sand pails and shovels lay half buried in worn-out sandboxes.

In the kitchen almond cookies had been arranged on a tray. A box of thick, many-colored candles sat beside the menorah, and a stack of blue-and-white-wrapped packages lay on a table near the door, their ribbons limp in the late-afternoon air. Jane stood before her mirror. Her dress was too long, but her hair had grown and was drawn back with two plastic barrettes.

A knock at the door. Sally appeared in a cotton dress printed with pale pink and yellow wildflowers. Winding through the pattern was a vine of green-and-white. A ruffled hem bounced above her knees, and she wore white knee-high stockings and black patent Mary Jane shoes. On her wrist was a delicate add-a-pearl bracelet.

"Oh, Sally, you look so wonderful. I love that dress."

"Thanks. Our dressmaker made it for tonight. Yours is nice too, Jane."

"Thank you."

Somehow Sally always made people feel good about themselves. Jane was trying to learn to do that, but she still blurted out remarks that seemed to hurt her friends. Why did she sound so cruel when she meant to be gentle?

"Come in now, girls," Mrs. Miller called. Mr. Miller had placed a yarmulke on his head, and now he handed one to Jeff. Grandpa, tall and angular in his best blue suit, walked into the living room.

"Papa, you remember Sally Garland?" said Mrs. Miller.

"Yes. How are you, Sally?" Grandpa turned to look warily at her. "Have you ever seen the candles lighted?"

"No, sir, this is my first time."

"And your parents gave you permission to come here?"

"Yes, sir." Sally was surprised.

"Good," replied Grandpa as he arranged the *tallis* over his shoulders and straightened his yarmulke. "We don't want any bad feelings here."

"Grandpa, why do you say that?" Jane cried.

But her mother gave a stern look, and Mr. Miller said quickly, "All right now, everyone, let us proceed."

They all gathered around the menorah, Sally looking slightly bewildered. Jane grasped her hand and squeezed it tight. Sally squeezed back, and they smiled down at their fingers. Mrs. Miller put a scarf over her hair as Jeff brought her a match already lit from the pilot light of the stove.

"Baruch ata Adonai Elohainu melech ha'olam asher kidshanu b'mitzvosav v'tzivanu l'hadlik ner shel Chanukah," sang Mrs. Miller as she lit the *shamos,* the leader candle, and then four more candles.

"Why four, Jane?" whispered Sally.

"It's the fourth night of Chanukah."

Everyone joined in on the "Amen," and there was clapping and embracing. Grandpa kissed Jane and Jeff and somewhat awkwardly shook Sally's hand. Mr. Miller hugged Jeff, enveloped Jane in a bear hug, and carefully kissed Mrs. Miller. "Happy Chanukah, Sally," he said. "I hope you'll come back on the other nights too."

"Thank you, Mr. Miller, I'd like to," she answered.

Mrs. Miller took Jane's face in her hands and kissed her on each cheek. "A good Chanukah to you, dear, and to you too, Sally." For a moment Jane felt an immense comfort, as if all the muscles around her heart had relaxed. Maybe someday her mother would sing in the kitchen or even smoke cigarettes and make jokes and call Jane's friends "cuties."

"Sally," said Mr. Miller, "have you any questions about all this?"

"Oh, yes, sir . . . why do you have eight candles?"

There was a grumble from Grandpa—an infidel was in their midst. Mrs. Miller, shooting a glance of warning at her father, put her hand on Sally's arm. "Because there was enough oil for only one day after the Jews regained the Temple, but there was a miracle and it burned instead for eight days."

"And then what happened?" she asked.

"They cleaned the Temple and rededicated it to God," said Jeff.

"You're lucky," said Sally. "Christmas is only for one measly day and then it's all over."

"Let's open the presents now," Jane said. "I can't wait any longer."

"Oh, Grandpa, this is just perfect." Jane lifted up eight long grosgrain ribbons of red and blue and yellow and orange. There was one of green, wider than the rest, with little silk flowers on the ends. She ran to her grandfather and kissed him. "How did you know I needed these?"

"Well, I travel all over the country, you know, and I see all these little girls with braids and ribbons, and I thought you might be wearing your hair that way someday. It would certainly be a lot better than that permanent your mother gave you."

"Papa!" Mrs. Miller turned from her package and stamped her foot.

"It's better for her hair to have that stuff out of it and just be natural."

Mr. Miller interrupted. "Jane, this is a wonderful bookmark. Now I don't have to use scraps of paper when I read. Thank you, honey."

He gave Mrs. Miller a silk scarf printed with birds and leaves. Jeff punched his fist into a plump leather baseball mitt, a gift from his parents, and Grandpa gave Mr. Miller a block of halvah, a sesame candy, from Chicago.

"My God, Papa, I haven't tasted this in a year. It's the best thing you could have brought. What a treat. Thanks a million—a million."

Grandpa, pleased, answered, "Down in this godforsaken place you can't buy halvah, can you? There's not even a delicatessen, is there? I thought you might really want this."

"Oh, I do, Papa . . . I really do. And I can't wait to eat it."

Sally gingerly unwrapped a narrow package. Nestling in the tissue paper was a thin pencil box with a snapped lid. In the box were three striped pencils, a rubber eraser, a compass, and a ruler. "Oh, thanks, everyone. My old pencil box is so tacky and I've lost the eraser. How did you know this is just what I needed?"

"Oh, we heard, we heard," answered Mr. Miller as Grandpa mumbled again and turned his head away.

"Time for a toast! Time for a toast! How about it?" asked Mrs. Miller.

"You have schnapps?" asked Grandpa.

"Of course, Papa, we always have schnapps for you," said Mr. Miller as he filled a shot glass. He poured out grape juice for the children.

"To health and love and Chanukah," said Mr. Miller, glancing at his wife.

"Yes," added Mrs. Miller. "And peace."

"L'chaim!" said Grandpa.

"Amen," said Jeff.

" 'I have a little dreidel, I made it out of clay . . . and when it's dry and ready, then dreidel I will play . . .' " Grandpa began to sing and dance around the room in bouncy steps, the fringes of his *tallis* flapping behind him.

" 'Oh, dreidel, dreidel, dreidel . . . I made it out of clay,' " sang Mrs. Miller as she followed behind her father, imitating his steps.

Mr. Miller held out his arms to Sally, and they waltzed about the room as he joined in: " 'Oh, dreidel, dreidel, dreidel . . .' "

Jeff and Jane, arms akimbo, did their idea of a Russian tsatzka. Everyone began to laugh, and gradually they fell into a loose circle, weaving in and out and touching hands as they passed one another. Furniture was shoved by flying bodies and kicking heels, and the menorah candles flickered furiously. But like the temple oil of Judas Maccabaeus, the candles refused to be extinguished and burned steadily.

It was almost like Chicago, thought Jane, when her uncles and aunts and countless cousins celebrated Chanukah at the Millers' house. The snow was usually on the ground by that time, and the front hall would be lined with galoshes. Piles of overcoats, still twinkling with snowflakes, would lie on the chairs.

They exchanged many, many presents. Everyone kissed everyone. Aunt Tilly always pinched all the children's cheeks too hard. Brilliant spots of red remained on their faces for at least half an hour afterward, making them look like a troupe of little clowns.

Mrs. Miller would have baked sponge cakes, waiting in the dining room. Margaret always set the table with a lace tablecloth and crystal candle holders, silverware from Tiffany's, and Wedgwood china. English serving plates, marking each place, would be whisked away as everyone sat down to dinner. Jane always wondered what possible use they served if no one was to eat from them. It would be better if the plates were already there, so that the potato *latkes* and applesauce could be served sooner.

After dinner, boxes of See's candy were opened and everyone searched for the ones with the caramel centers. Grandpa had brought each of the children a net bag of gold-wrapped chocolate coins. "Here is your Chanukah *gelt,*" he would say as he held the presents above his head. "All you have to do is give me a kiss."

"But Grandpa," the cousins would all declare in mock distress, "your mustache is so scratchy!"

"Ah, yes indeed, it is," said Grandpa, doing his bouncy jog. "But you know what the Torah says, don't you?"

"Yes, Grandpa!" They shouted together, the boys and girls giggling and clutching one another as they hopped up and down for their candy money.

"The Torah says," teased Grandpa, "a kiss without a mustache—"

"—is like an egg without salt!" screamed the children as they all rushed forward to hug his knees and kiss him and reach for the shiny bags he held in his hands.

Here in Corpus Christi the musty odor of the furniture rose as they moved round the room, and in the kitchen, Jane knew, was a very plain dinner.

But her mother had taken off her headband, so that her hair was loose and moving freely. And she was smiling a little. Daddy was actually laughing as he carefully placed the treasured halvah on the coffee table, and Jeff was whirling Sally in the air.

Jane stopped as a knifelike fear struck her. Jeff would go to war. She would be left alone without him. But at least Grandpa was there for a while and Daddy had made a little money this week and she had eight new, heavy grosgrain ribbons for her hair.

Chapter 19

F riday was the sixth night of Chanukah. The menorah, six candles in place for the evening lighting, was on the dining-room sideboard. Jeff and Jane sat on spread-out newspapers as they rubbed the Friday-night candlesticks, the kiddush cup, and the bread dish with silver paste and old, soft cloths.

From the kitchen came the smells of a brisket baking in the oven and chicken soup simmering. A darkened sky and growing winds warned of a cold, wet norther blowing in from the Panhandle of Texas. Prayerbook in hand, Grandpa suddenly loomed over them.

"Did anyone turn off the light in the icebox?"

"Sorry, Papa, we forgot," called Mrs. Miller from her bedroom.

"Jeff, will you please do that?" asked Grandpa. "If anyone opens that icebox door and God sees the light go

131

on, both He and I will be very upset. And during Chanukah especially—oh, my God."

"Even the *icebox* light?" asked Jane.

"Jane, when God said that no one will work and that no one will turn on a light during *Shabbos,* He meant *all* lights."

"But the sun hasn't set yet, Papa." Mrs. Miller came into the room.

"But in an hour it will, and we must all think ahead. You know that preparations have to be finished in time."

Jeff jumped up and went into the kitchen. "Okay, Grandpa, it's done." He came back, sat down, and picked up a clean cloth.

"Thank you, Jeff." Grandpa went into his room and came out with a small overnight case. "Good-bye, everyone. I'll see you on Saturday night," he said as he opened the front door. He put the worn prayerbook under his arm, close to his heart.

"Papa, where do you think you're going?"

"I'm going to *shul.* Why do you ask such ridiculous questions? It's Friday night and it's time to pray. Just because there's a church on every corner, do you think that God doesn't know it's *Shabbos*?"

"Calm down, Papa," said Mrs. Miller, trying to take the bag from him. "I know it's *Shabbos,* but eat dinner first, and we'll get a neighbor to drive you to *shul.*"

"*Drive . . . me . . . to . . .* shul? *Drive . . . me . . . to . . .* shul?"

"For pity's sake, Papa, you can't walk eight miles in this heat."

"*Drive. Drive me to* shul?"

"Papa, stop yelling. God will forgive a seventy-three-year-old man if he accepts a ride in a car *once* on a Friday night. Besides, the sun hasn't gone down yet—technically. We can eat dinner at six and ask Mr. Berman to come and pick you up."

"I don't want to ride in anyone's car. Besides, I like to walk. That illiterate newspaper of yours gave sundown today at five thirty-three. If that's true, and I doubt it highly, that will give me two hours—"

"Papa, let's call your rabbi and ask."

"There's a big storm coming," said Jeff.

"Papa, you are so damned stubborn."

"Ruth, you're still my daughter. Please don't speak to me that way."

"But Grandpa," said Jane, "we'll be driving to temple with the Wiles at seven-thirty. Come with us."

"All of you leave me alone. You are Reform Jews, which I can just about tolerate, but I refuse to ride in your cars or write or turn on lights or work—and you know it. Do things your way, but have a little respect for me." He turned to open the screen door.

"But Papa, are you going to walk home in the dark and then walk back for services tomorrow morning? Louis will have a fit. Can't you tell there's a storm coming?" Mrs. Miller clutched at the back of her father's coat.

"What's the matter with this family? I can take care of myself. I've arranged everything."

Grandpa threw open the door and started down the two steps. Jeff tried to grab him too, but Mrs. Miller was in his way. Mr. Leigh, who was cleaning a catch of fish in his front yard, ran over and reached out to Grandpa. "Whoa there, Mr. Brodin, don't fall."

"I don't intend to," said Grandpa.

He broke loose and loped toward the road. Jeff ran after him but slammed into Mr. Leigh.

"Papa, *stop!*" called Mrs. Miller. She came down the steps. "Somebody go after him, *please!*" Jane and Jeff pursued him, with Mr. Leigh trailing behind.

"Why are we running?" Mr. Leigh was panting.

"We're trying to keep him from walking into town," called Jeff over his shoulder.

Mr. Leigh nodded and puffed forward. "Papa!" called Mrs. Miller. "Where will you stay?"

"I'm spending the night at the rabbi's house," yelled Grandpa as he reached the grassy shoulder of the highway. "Tomorrow I'm walking to services with him."

Jane ran beside Grandpa. "Did you take a toothbrush? Do you have pajamas?"

"Janie, you worry me." He strode forward. "A good Jew makes sure he is a good Jew. I have everything packed for the night. Now, all of you leave me alone! Good-bye." He waved them off as if they were gnats.

"At least take the rabbi's wife a little gift," called Mrs. Miller. She stopped to clutch her side.

"I've taken her a scarf!" He walked even faster.

"But Mr. Brodin," said Mr. Leigh, "it's so hot!"

"Enough . . . all of you. If God thought we could get to *shul* another way on *Shabbos,* He would have provided silver wings."

Mr. Leigh sat down, perspiring, by the side of the

road. Jeff and Jane trotted beside Grandpa. His black coat flapped against Jane's legs.

Faster he strode, a tall and bony figure leaning forward, his mustache flattening in the wind. His eyes shone. Set against the red and pink azalea bushes and the blue-gray water of the bay, his billowing black coat made him look like a figure in a painting by El Greco that Jane had seen in a book. There had been a shimmering connection from the man's body to the heavens above, and Grandpa seemed surrounded by the same light now.

Cars were slowing down. "Excuse me," said a large woman in a blue car. "Like a ride into town?"

"Grandpa," said Jeff, "go with her."

"No, thank you," replied Grandpa. "It's a day for me to walk, but thank you very much."

"Whatever you say," answered the driver as she moved away. Three blond children pointed out the back window at them.

A farm truck stopped. "Goin' into town?" the driver called.

"Grandpa, please take this one. We'll go with you," said Jane.

"No, thank you, sir. Kind of you to ask," Grandpa said.

"Suit yourself, sir." The motor gunned.

A navy jeep and a rattly Ford were slowing down. Loud honking as Ocean Drive became blocked. Cows in the nearby field looked up.

Finally Jeff and Jane fell back. Grandpa moved swiftly away from them into the sun, a huge red ball that outlined his figure in flames.

Chapter 20

The last day of Chanukah was stifling hot. That morning Grandpa and Jane's mother had had a terrible argument:

"Papa, I am always having to wipe up after you in the bathroom. Can't you be more careful?"

"Ruth, I'll try, but it gets difficult when you grow older. You know . . . an old violin—"

"Papa, please don't make jokes. You leave the sink a mess."

"Oh, I do? Sorry, really."

"And you never wash out the tub. Please clean up after yourself."

"Of course I will. How about a little kiss? A kiss without a mustache—"

"Papa, *please*! It's hard enough to get things done around here. Please don't make me be your maid. I am not a maid."

Grandpa's cheeks had rippled as he tried to do a little dance after Mrs. Miller left the room.

How could her mother speak that way to Grandpa . . . to her own father? Didn't she remember that he was even poorer than they were? Ever since Grandma had died five years earlier, Grandpa had wandered around the country. He had no permanent home. Didn't she see that he was trying to hold on to his dignity, in his threadbare suit and worn, enormous shoes?

Jane wanted to run and embrace him. But if she did, he would know that she had recognized his embarrassment. So she pretended to straighten the curtains.

Grandpa sat down. He gazed at the carpet, his bald spot pale and damp. His hands were clasped tightly together. After a moment he said, "So, little girl, what do you say? A little whirl into town? I could use the company."

"Okay, Grandpa. What are you going to do?"

"I'm visiting a very classy but slightly stuffy establishment, which needs my wares. And afterward I'll let you buy some ice cream."

"Will you have some too?"

"Kosher ice cream in Corpus Christi, Texas?"

"Sorry."

As she put on her cotton dress she was still upset. Did other people feel things this way? It was as if she saw hundreds of strings crisscrossing the room, and these spider-web-like things entrapped and hurt her mother and father, or sometimes Jeff or Grandpa. Maybe she would get caught herself. If she got caught, maybe she would never get away, never get free.

Jane and Grandpa stood in front of Browning, McCall, Ltd., Men's Furnishings. Through the sweating windows they saw polite displays of gingham shirts with pearl buttons, cotton-twill jackets, and silk ties. Off to the side were a silver-encrusted saddle and a pair of cowboy boots.

Grandpa pushed open the door and they entered the cool gloom. Wooden fans spun overhead. Jane drew a grateful breath. Perspiration rolled down inside the back of her dress as Grandpa placed his case upon the gleaming counter.

"Yes, sir, can I help you?" asked an alarmed-looking man in a blue suit with a matching vest.

"I would like to show you my goods, sir."

"We buy directly from Houston and New York, although I'm sure you must have very nice things. I am Dan Browning. Perhaps we can make this another time," he said as he tried to steer Grandpa and Jane toward the door.

For an instant Grandpa looked frightened. Jane glanced up at pictures of cattle round-ups, campfires, and horses rearing.

"Just one minute, Mr. Browning, that's all I ask." Grandpa tried to undo the snaps of his sample case.

"Excuse me, sir, but our merchandise is ordered for next season, and other things are made to measure. I'm sure you understand—"

"One minute, that's all. Just let me show you the ties. You have nothing like them in your store."

"I'm sure we don't," said Mr. Browning. Dusty rays of sun through the window shone around Grandpa's white hair.

"What's happening here?" Another man appeared.

"This is my partner, John McCall," said Mr. Browning. "John, I was just telling, uh, your name, sir?"

"Leon Brodin. I have very fine things from Chicago."

"I was just telling Mr. . . . Brodin that we have our regular suppliers."

"Well, let's all go in the back, where it's cooler," said Mr. McCall.

"Fine, fine, gentlemen. You won't be sorry," said Grandpa as he picked up his case and held it close to his chest. Jane followed into the storeroom crowded with packing boxes and piles of paper and string.

"Let's see what you have, sir," said Mr. Browning.

"Yes, right away. Oh, this is my granddaughter, Jane."

"How do you do, Jane," answered the men. One of them flashed an irritable look at Grandpa.

She wanted to scream at them. But she made herself sit down on a crate and try to pull her short dress over her scabby knees.

"Now here are handkerchiefs, hand-rolled, as you can see . . . monogrammed and all." Grandpa draped the squares over his arm and held them up to the light.

"We monogram only on order, Mr. Brodin. What else can you show us?"

"Well, how about these ties? Very colorful, very up-to-the-minute. I have them in all patterns—striped, dotted, paisley."

"I think not, sir. Our customers prefer quieter ties."

Grandpa sighed, and Jane could see his knees dip as he clung to the table edge and reached into his case again.

"Yes, of course. But look at these bow ties. Now I didn't see any outside, and these are very smart."

Mr. Browning took the tie from Grandpa. "John," he said, "we never carry those."

"Well, why don't we give it a try for once?" asked Mr. McCall, glancing at his partner.

"Oh, yes, of course," said Mr. Browning. "Yes, well, let's have this blue one and the two with the dots and the striped one. How about that?"

"How much are they?" asked Mr. McCall.

"For you, only one dollar fifty apiece. I usually sell them for—"

"Yes, thank you." Mr. Browning took some money from a box on the desk. Grandpa's head bent lower and lower as he neatly placed the bills inside his wallet. But then he straightened and said, "Thank you, gentlemen. This has not been easy for any of us, but I'm proud of what I sell, and I thank you for buying it."

Mr. McCall flushed slightly but looked steadily at Grandpa. Jane stood up and took Grandpa's cuff. He smiled down at her.

Finally Mr. Browning replied, "You are welcome, sir. And it was nice to meet you and Jane."

"Thank you, and God give you all His blessings," added Grandpa as he closed the case and adjusted his yarmulke.

"Yes, sir, thank you," Mr. McCall said. "I'm sure the bow ties will do well." He led the way back into the showroom.

"Sorry we can't do more, but we hope you understand," said Mr. Browning.

"Indeed, yes. Thank you for coming . . . and we hope you enjoy Corpus Christi." Mr. McCall held the door open.

"I will, thank you. I will be coming back every year," said Grandpa.

"Good-bye, Mr. Brodin," said Mr. McCall as Jane and Grandpa left the store.

The harsh light outside made them squint and cover their eyes. For a few blocks Grandpa remained upright, but as they neared the bus stop he clutched the handle of his case. His breathing was slow, and once he stopped and peered down at the curb, as if something might grow up from there and give him strength. At last he lifted his head and continued walking. As they passed Lichtenstein's Department Store and the bus approached, Jane slipped her hand into his.

Chapter 21

E very day when the school bus dropped Jane
at the tourist court, she locked the door of
her room, pulled down all the shades, and
gently drew the tree from its hiding place in the closet.

As she plugged in the lights a glow suffused the room
and seemed to fill the cracked walls and cover the linoleum with a blue light, like a Picasso painting of two little
boys she had once seen. One boy was tall and thin, his
arms crossed and resting on his waist, and the other boy
was smaller and chubby, dressed in darker clothes. The
children seemed to be waiting for something as they each
looked in a different direction on the beige, tree-laced
landscape. Was someone coming to get them, to take care
of them? Would they go home? Now, turning slowly in
the blue room, Jane remembered the patient little boys.

She wiggled under the tree, her head touching the
metal stand, her eyes squinting upward through the

branches. Is this what it's like to be Episcopalian? To wear black Mary Janes and knee-high white stockings? To have a mother who drinks Cokes and arranges poinsettias in a china pot from Neiman-Marcus?

This tree was beautiful, but so were Friday-night dinners with the *Shabbos* candles and the silver kiddush cup.

One day she would live in her own bright, spacious house. It would have a curved stairway leading up to the second floor. She might travel. Wasn't there something better than getting married? Jane would never be like her parents. She would go someplace wonderful, far away, the minute she was old enough.

The blue lights and the shining ornaments, the paper birds, and strings of popcorn blended with the cranberries . . . whirling, changing, growing lighter, then darker as spears of light pierced her vision and then turned into spots and circles and stars . . .

When Jane was five and had gone to the hospital to have her tonsils out, the doctor had placed a cone over her face. As she breathed in and out she began to move backward into vibrant spirals of color. Touching the fragrant branches now and squeezing her eyes almost shut, she could hear the voice of Dr. Stern saying, "Count for me, Janie. Count for me. Can you count backward?"

As a sharp pine needle brushed across her forehead she was once more being wheeled down the hall toward the operating room. Her mother held her hand and her father walked beside the gurney. Suddenly her parents stopped as the stretcher continued down the hall.

"Mommy, don't leave. Where am I going?" she had cried.

"Now, Jane, be a brave girl. You'll be just fine," said Mrs. Miller.

"Daddy, come with me, please."

"Don't cry, honey. We'll be right here when you come out." Mr. Miller had waved as he and Mrs. Miller became tiny figures in the wide corridor. . . .

She opened her eyes and looked up into the tree with its ever-changing patterns and dots and dashes of light in the darkening room.

Each night as the Millers placed the menorah in the window, Jane found it painful to breathe, as if someone had pressed a hand onto her chest. As she recited the prayers and watched the brave little menorah candles burst into flame, she knew that her grandfather would never forgive her if he found the tree. He had brought her barrettes for her hair and socks with embroidered flowers on the cuffs and a bracelet with rhinestones and a book about Chanukah. She had made a leather bookmark for him and a quilted holder for his glasses.

"Kiss me, Janie," he had cried. "Kiss me right now. I love my present, and you know . . . a kiss without a mustache—"

"—is like an egg without salt." She sighed as she had thrown her arms around Grandpa's neck.

He always smelled of herring and hard-boiled eggs and the schnapps, which he drank every night before dinner. And now on his lapels and tie were food stains, which he didn't seem to notice. It was suffocating in his arms, but she loved him too.

"Grandpa, that's enough, that's enough. Let me go."

"I will if you give me one more kiss."

"All right . . . *here!*" One more kiss. She saw another spot on his suit. Was this what it was like to grow old? She would never be like that.

"And you, Jeff . . ." Grandpa had beckoned with his knotty finger. "You may be old enough to battle Hitler, but you are not too old to kiss your grandfather."

"I know, Grandpa. A kiss without a mustache—"

"—is like an egg without salt!" A triumphant cry as Jeff bent down.

Jane reached up and pulled down a pine needle. It smelled bitter and fresh.

When school had let out for Christmas, she put away her silk dresses and brown shoes and spent the days in unironed shorts and polo shirts, just like Sally's. Her feet became callused and hard.

Grandpa had once more taken over the routine of the Miller household. When he prayed, at least twenty times a day, his *tallis* and *t'fillin* in place, all other activities ceased. The chanting singsong of his *davening* filled the house; and if Jane or Jeff should hurtle into the room where he was swaying back and forth at the east-facing wall, they froze instantly like deer caught in the headlights of a car. Without losing a word of his prayer, Grandpa would turn around and cast a warning eye upon them as Moses must have when he came down from the mountain after having spoken to God. Beneath the prayers was the message: *Do not move one inch or I will never forgive you.*

The telephone went unanswered, the tea kettle whistled, and friends waited outside the door until Grandpa was done. Slowly he folded the silk scarf and unwound the leather straps from his arms. Once he had placed them in the blue velvet case, with the gold Star of David embroidered on it they could continue on to whatever unimportant place they had been going.

After dinner he would sit in the living room, his feet on the hassock, and read old Yiddish newspapers that he had brought from Chicago. The tattered papers hid his face, so that only the worn bottoms of his enormous shoes and the tip of his yarmulke showed.

While he read, Jane did her homework on the dining room table. One evening Jeff and two friends entered the living room.

"Grandpa, I'd like to introduce Leslie Coleman and Ben Chernuck."

"Uhmm . . ." A rustle of the paper, but no face appeared.

"Grandpa, Ben is—"

"How do you do, sir."

"Which one is Ben?" Two eyes barely showed.

"I am, sir."

"You're in the navy?" The paper was lowered halfway.

"Coast Guard, sir."

"You're Jewish?"

"Uh . . . uh . . . half Jewish, sir."

"*Oy.*" Up went the paper again.

"And this is Leslie, Grandpa."

"Is she Jewish?"

"Ah . . . no, sir," said Leslie.

"Oh, my God."

The children looked at one another, uncomfortably.

Leslie said, "Well, it was nice to meet you, sir" as she tugged at Jeff's hand.

"Good-bye, sir," said Ben as he turned to go.

A grunt from behind the paper.

They backed out of the living room.

Jane sighed and went back to her homework. Did Grandpa have to be so stubborn, so mean? Didn't he know how hard it was to make friends here, particularly since there were so few Jewish children their own ages? Ben would be leaving for the war soon, and Grandpa had treated him like a criminal! Sometimes it seemed as if Grandpa was their worst enemy.

During vacation Sally and Jane had gone crabbing off the Garlands' pier. Josephine packed them a lunch of tuna fish sandwiches, with pickles, celery, and jalapeño peppers mixed into the mayonnaise. She included a thermos of iced tea, cookies wrapped in waxed paper, and a pile of napkins left over from the Christmas party.

The two girls dropped their baited strings over the edge of the dock and waited. They covered themselves with an orange mixture of baby oil and iodine and stretched out in the sun, the splintery boards edging into their backs.

"Jane, why won't your grandpa let you eat crabs?"

Jane paused. "Um . . . because," she said carefully, "in our religion they're considered . . . unclean."

"But why?"

"Shellfish eat everything in the sea. They don't select carefully, so they're kind of . . . bad food. Grandpa calls them *traife*."

"But everybody eats those things."

"But they didn't in the olden days, in biblical times, you know, because they didn't have iceboxes and stuff like that."

"Who told you that?"

"We learned it in Sunday school. And Grandpa reminds us of it all the time."

"I'll bet he does! But don't you even get to eat one teeny little shrimp or clam when no one is looking?"

"Oh, sure, when we have them at school for lunch. And sometimes Daddy takes me to the Greek café in his building. But we don't tell Mother."

One night, lying under her tree, Jane had heard a country song from next door: "All day I face the barren waste, without the taste of water . . . cool water." The Sons of the Pioneers were singing, their close harmony sending the soothing melody through the window: "Old Dan and I with throats burned dry and souls that cry for water . . . cool, clear water."

In the Miller living room the radio announcer was talking about the war, the war, the war. Everyone seemed sad and upset all the time. Mr. Miller kept a map pinned to the wall, and every time there was a new development, he took little colored pins and marked areas in Poland, France, and Germany and in places Jane had never heard of before: Iwo Jima, Okinawa, Saipan.

Lying in her room, she knew that he and her mother and Grandpa would be clustered around the radio, their heads next to the speaker. Jeff would be looking up from his schoolwork, a frown on his face.

Jane tried to sing along with the country music. She liked these tales of love and death and divorce played on mournful, wailing guitars and violins. "Keep a-movin', Dan, don't you listen to the man. He's a devil, not a man, and he spreads the burning sand with water . . . cool, clear water." But the announcer's words seeped under the door.

"There is terrible suffering along the Russian front."

She knew what was happening in Russia, where many of her aunts and uncles and cousins still lived, but she wasn't even sure exactly where Europe was! In geography class she could never remember which sides of maps were east, west, north, or south. Her tutor in Chicago had told her that, in time, she would be able to "see" a map, but Mr. Penn gave her very bad grades.

A loud knock on the door jerked Jane from her reverie under the tree, so that a pine needle almost went into her eye. She lay back down and rubbed it.

"Janie, what are you doing in there?" Grandpa was saying.

"I'll be right out, Grandpa." Slowly, slowly she began to slide forward from under the branches.

Another knock. "Open the door, Jane. I want to speak with you."

Did he suspect something? "Grandpa, I will. In just one minute." She unplugged the cord and began to push the tree back into the closet. It tilted, the tinsel and the ornaments dangling.

"Jane, you are being rude. I would like a cup of tea, please. Your mother is not feeling well, and you know I have my tea now."

"Yes, Grandpa, I'll be right there." She lifted the tree and moved it toward the closet. One more push.

"And Jane, there is some cake the rabbi's wife sent over."

The knock forced open the weak latch on the door. Grandpa, surprised, stood with his hand raised to knock again.

She was hot. Her hands came up to cover her face, and even in her panic, she knew that she must look like Eve caught by God after eating the apple in the Garden of Eden.

Grandpa said, "I'm so sorry, I didn't mean to . . ." Then he looked down and saw the quivering tree. His mouth opened slightly and seemed to freeze. Jane's foot knocked against the base of the tree, and it swayed crazily. The country music from next door ricocheted off the walls as Grandpa's breathing grew louder.

"This is not possible," Grandpa whispered.

"Please, it doesn't mean—"

"You have this heathen thing—"

"Grandpa, please let me try to explain—"

"Ah-h-h-h-h-h" came a cry from Grandpa. Then another *"ah-h-h-h-h-h"* as he clutched his chest.

Jane rushed toward him, and the tree fell over on its side. She tried to steady him. "Please, Grandpa, it's not so bad . . ."

But he lowered his forehead into one hand and grasped the door frame with the other.

"Please don't be mad at me, Grandpa. It's not so terrible."

"Oh, God, oh, God . . . oh, my God," he moaned.

Mr. and Mrs. Miller were standing in the doorway behind him. Jeffrey slipped under his arm and into the room.

"Oh, my God, what have you done?" cried Grandpa.

"Grandpa, stop . . . please stop. Let us talk to you," pleaded Jeff.

"Papa, come into the living room," said Mr. Miller, pulling on his sleeve.

Grandpa raised his hand and made himself look at the tree. Uttering strange words—half Yiddish and half Polish—he flew into Jane's room like a wounded, flapping stork, his black coat opening and spreading apart like wings. He moved from one side of the room to the other.

Finally he bent down and grabbed the tree by its trunk. Around and around he swung it, high over his head, ornaments crashing to the floor, berries and popcorn careening into space, and light bulbs popping like balloons. He pounded the tree into the rug again and again, until it splintered into jagged pieces.

Jeff crouched and tried to grab his hands. "Grandpa, put it down, put it down," he called. But the pounding continued.

Jane started to weep. "Please, Grandpa, stop. I'm so sorry, I'm so sorry . . . just let me talk to you."

He lifted the tree even higher, drew back his arm, and threw it at the window above Jane's bed. Glass shattered over the sheets and the spread.

"Jane, Jeff, cover your eyes," Mrs. Miller cried.

"Papa, stop this. You're going to kill yourself," shouted Mr. Miller. "Children, watch out!"

He tried to enter, but Grandpa lunged at him and screamed, "Get out!" He turned and fixed his gaze upon Jane.

"Oh, God, I knew this would happen," said Mrs. Miller, hiding her face in her husband's shoulder. "He's going to hurt her. He's going to go mad!" She tried to reach Jane, but Grandpa flung out his arm and pushed her aside.

Grandpa moved toward Jane in one giant step. Picking her up by the waist, he violently shook her as if she were a Raggedy Ann doll. He shouted, "You are an infidel! An infidel! God will punish you for this!"

The room was a blur through her terrified tears.

Jeff yelled, "Grandpa, put her down!"

"Papa, stop!" begged Mrs. Miller.

Grandpa lifted Jane back and to the side, as if he were winding up to throw a ball. Mrs. Miller screamed as Jane's legs dangled.

"No! No!" they all shouted.

And then Grandpa started to cry. "Oh, God, forgive me, forgive me," he said, and lowered her slowly to the floor, where she fell into a heap at his feet. "Oh, forgive me," he said again as he blindly pushed everyone aside, stumbled into the living room, and ran onto the front lawn, the screen door banging behind him.

Mrs. Miller kneeled and took Jane into her arms. "It's all right. You'll be all right."

"Are you hurt, Janie?" asked Mr. Miller, sitting on the floor and smoothing the damp hair away from her eyes.

Jeff cradled her bare feet in his hands. "It's okay, Jane, the worst is over . . . it's over."

The Sons of the Pioneers were still singing and the radio announcer was saying something about General Eisenhower and his army. The family clung together in the shadowy room. It was Christmas Day, 1944.

Chapter 22

Two days after the discovery of the tree the house was still very quiet. Grandpa would not speak. Jane felt as if someone had died. She was beginning to think everyone was mourning for her. Why else were people ignoring her?

Sally was in East Texas visiting her grandparents, so each day Jane went down to a secluded place on the beach and sat with her arms around her knees. Hiding her face, she peered down into the sand shaded by her legs and drew circles within circles within circles. Sometimes she jumped up and down to try to throw off the sad feelings, but nothing worked.

Food tasted like sawdust now. Over and over she saw her grandfather hurl the tree across the room and felt his hands gripping her waist as he lifted her into the air.

She must find a way to tell Grandpa that the tree had made her feel, for a little while, that she was like all her friends in this new town. She wanted to tell him that she was sorry—that she loved him and didn't want to lose him from her life. If Jeffrey left for the army, who would protect her? Who would love her and tell her stories? She wanted to talk to Grandpa, sit on his lap, and put her head under his chin as he sang his songs.

If he left now, without ever speaking to her again, that might cut her off forever from all her relatives in Chicago. They would be furious, too, that she had had a tree. Then she would be a person without a past. Without aunts and uncles and cousins and even second and third cousins, third cousins like the Izbickis, who had come over from Poland a year ago and were just learning to speak English.

If she died of remorse, would her mother cry? Would Daddy miss her? And would Grandpa understand, as she was being lowered into the ground, that she really had been a good person and hadn't meant to hurt anyone?

* * *

"Jeffrey, you can't imagine what a battle is really like, in the trenches, crawling around with a gun on your back."

"I know, Dad, really . . . I mean, I don't know, but it's getting worse now, and if they'll take me—"

"They won't, Jeff," said his father. "And even if they wanted to, you have to finish high school first."

The Millers were having sabbath dinner. The candles had burned halfway down, and the braided challah bread was almost gone. Grandpa sat silently as he cut his food into exact, tiny pieces. Jane stared at her plate. Maybe the meat and the string beans would melt into the printed kimonoed ladies and Japanese bridges and vanish into the land of uneaten meals.

"But Dad, how can you discourage me like this? You keep talking about Hitler and Hirohito and this whole nightmare, but you want to keep me at home."

"I'm not saying that, Jeff. I just mean that if you—"

"I'm leaving," interrupted Grandpa.

"Leaving for where?" asked Mr. Miller.

"I made reservations on the train for Thursday, and I'm leaving. Mel and Burt will meet me in Chicago."

"Grandpa, you can't do that," cried Jane, shifting her position to kneel in her chair.

"Jane, sit properly," warned Mrs. Miller.

"I've torn my shirt. You are all dead to me. I'm leaving."

Jane's face began to crumple into tears.

"Grandpa, if you'd just listen for a minute," said Jeff.

"I do not have to listen to infidels." Grandpa stood up and pushed back his chair. "If my own children defy the laws of the Torah and care nothing for the feelings of their grandfather . . . if they care nothing for God—"

"But we do care, Grandpa." Jane was on her knees again and almost crawling onto the table. "Is God so mean that He doesn't forgive a mistake? Doesn't He understand at all? What I did is not so terrible."

"You put something in your house, a Christian symbol —only *worse*. It comes from Germany . . . *Germany*! That Christmas tree comes from *Germany,* and you talk about right and wrong, Louis, and 'good' wars and 'bad' wars."

"Papa," cried Mr. Miller, "we're sorry. We're all so sorry. You're right! You're right! We admit that."

"How could you have brought that vile thing into the house?" Grandpa's fist crashed onto the tablecloth, which pulled to one side. A serving dish flew to the floor and sprayed peas and carrots all over the carpet. Jane jumped from her chair and backed up against the wall.

"From *Germany*! From *Hitler*! *Traife*! *Traife*! God will never forgive you! I will never forgive you!"

"Papa, we knew it was wrong," cried Mrs. Miller, trying to grab Grandpa's hand, but he shook her off and moved away. "We were ambivalent from the beginning, really, Papa . . . really—" she continued.

"*Ambivalent*?" interrupted Grandpa, his yarmulke askew, "*Ambivalent*? A very fancy word for betraying God!"

Mr. Miller stood up. "It is not a betrayal, Papa."

"Yes, it is . . . it is," said Grandpa as he moved back and forth across the dining room, like an animal trying to destroy its cage. "It is a betrayal of God and of me. You betrayed *me*!"

Jane gasped. *Betrayed Grandpa?* He sounded just like Mother. She was always making things personal like that. How could he think such a stupid thing? Jane turned her head and looked out the window. Except, really, they had betrayed him. They had known what being a Jew meant to him. She should never have had that little tree.

"We did not," Jeff was saying. "We love you, Grandpa."

"We made a mistake, Papa," said Mr. Miller as he sat down with a weary sigh.

"*Worse! Worse!*" shouted the old man. "You did much worse than that."

"Listen to me, Papa," said Mr. Miller. "We did it because we wanted to give her something—"

"She is a Jewish girl." Grandpa whirled around and pointed a finger at Mr. Miller. "She has her religion."

"Yes, of course she does, and she'll always have it," said Mr. Miller. "But right now she's a stranger here. I took her away from her friends and her family, and she's having a very hard time."

"So did Judas Maccabaeus when he fought off his enemies and entered a filthy temple."

"But she's a little girl, Papa," interjected Mrs. Miller.

"Judas Maccabaeus was just a young man, but he led the Jews into battle to fight for their religion," shouted Grandpa. "He took up weapons . . . a Jew who would fight to the death for his faith. We celebrate the Feast of Lights in his honor. We do not celebrate Christmas!"

"Papa!" Mr. Miller held up his hands. "Judas Maccabaeus is no match for Santa Claus. Put them up against each other, and Judas Maccabaeus will lose every time."

"Blasphemy! You are speaking blasphemy! You have failed as a Jewish father."

"We have to live our lives, Papa," answered Mr. Miller. "This little girl needed something of her own. I can't give her clothes and parties and new friends. I wanted to give her . . . a gift."

"The wrong gift is what you gave her," yelled Grandpa. He knocked over the chair. "You have given gifts until you went bankrupt. You gave my daughter too much . . . cars, coats, maids—"

"She deserved them, Papa."

"Nobody's saying she didn't. But you stole money to pay for them. You can never say no to anyone. That's weakness, Lou."

"Grandpa," said Jane, "please don't yell at Daddy."

"I *will* yell! Your father has made too many mistakes. You, too, Ruth—you wanted luxuries, you know you did. This tree is the worst mistake, a *shanda*. You've shamed me."

Mr. Miller's eyes grew wide and shiny. "Papa, I wanted to give her . . ." His voice seemed to catch in his throat. "I wanted her to have . . ." But he stopped speaking and turned away.

Jeff circled the table to comfort him as Mrs. Miller said, "I *told* you so! I *told* you this would happen! But no one listened to me. No one *ever* listens to me!"

Jane ran into to her bedroom. They did not notice she had gone.

Chapter 23

Grandpa was sitting in one of the metal chairs outside the door beside his suitcases. It was the last day of Chanukah. Jane was washing the beach sand from her feet with the hose. From almost all the cottages came the tense, rapid voice of the radio announcer. Mr. Miller walked down the front stairs.

"Papa, are you all right?"

Grandpa did not seem to hear, though—the sound of splashing made him turn around in his chair. Jane caught his glance, dull and full of pain. How lonely he looks, she thought, and I'm the cause of it all.

Grandpa still did not speak, but he drew a wrinkled handkerchief from his pants pocket and wiped his eyes. Mr. Miller gently placed his wide hand upon Grandpa's shoulder. For a moment Grandpa seemed to move back into the comfort of the touch. But then he bent forward and lowered his head as he wiped his red and swollen eyes. Mr. Miller went back inside.

Rumbling sounds of trucks came from the highway. Sailors clustered together in the open back of one truck, their round hats barely showing above the slatted sides. The voices of children playing near the boats babbled up to the top of the steps.

"Grandpa . . ."

Grandpa held up his hand as if to stop her. Jane turned off the hose tightly and went into the house.

Mrs. Miller, looking strangely unkempt, was standing at the kitchen sink. Jane looked at her. How could everyone stay so angry? She opened the icebox door and removed an apple.

Mrs. Miller snapped, "Jane, go outside and get that sand off. How many times do I have to tell you?"

Someone was actually talking to her. "But Mother, I did . . . I swear I did. Look, my feet are still a little bit wet."

"All I see is sand between your toes and on your legs and you are ruining my kitchen floor and—" Mrs. Miller burst into tears, her voice rising as she wept. "And now look what you've done. You've upset me completely. I work so hard in this house, and you don't . . ." More tears as she looked out the back window and wiped her eyes with her apron.

"Mother, I'm sorry. I'm sorry, really. I'll go outside and do it again."

"No, never mind, never mind. You never do anything I ask. Oh, God . . . *God* . . . why can't you cooperate just a little bit?"

That edge to her mother's voice. Jane backed away and pressed against the sink in preparation for the final crescendo, which she knew would send her reeling as if she had actually been hit in the face. Could she ever make her mother love her? "Are you so mad about the tree?" she yelled. "Are you going to treat me like this for the rest of my life?"

"Oh, Jane, Janie . . . I'm sorry." Mrs. Miller crossed the room and embraced her. "I'm sorry, really I am. It's not the tree—at least, I mean, not this minute."

"Well, what is it, then?" How strange to be hugged after not having been touched for days. Jane gradually adjusted her body to her mother's. But somewhere, spinning little dotted lines in her head, was the fear that at any moment Mrs. Miller might move away and start screaming again.

"I can't tell you what's happening right now, Janie. I just can't."

"Why not?"

"Because you're too little and we don't want to upset you. Besides, you wouldn't understand. Please don't ask me anymore."

"I'm not so stupid, Mother. *Tell me!*"

Mrs. Miller separated herself from Jane. "No, honey, I can't. Now go get that sand off and take your bath. You have to set the table and you're late."

Mr. Miller walked into the kitchen. "What is it now, Ruth? What's the matter? What's wrong, Jane?"

"I don't know, *dammit*! No one will tell me anything and everyone knows something that I don't and no one will talk to me—and *I hate you all!*"

"Jane, how dare you speak like that!" Mr. Miller's eyes grew red.

Jane's heart beat fast. "I'm sorry, Daddy, really . . . but—"

"How can you say you hate your own parents?" cried Mrs. Miller.

Jane began to feel tears breaking through, but her father raised his hand. "Stop that crying, Jane, or I will really give you something to cry about."

"Daddy, is it the tree? Why won't anyone even say good morning to me? I can't be as bad as all that."

"It's not just the tree, Jane," said Mr. Miller.

"Well, I've tried to talk to Grandpa and tell him I'm sorry, but he won't even look at me."

"No, Jane, it's more than that." Mr. Miller paused for a very long time and looked at her. "We've had some extremely bad news, and we don't want to talk about it right now. We don't even know if we can believe it . . . so we're just waiting for more information."

"Will you tell me later?"

"We'll see."

"I *hate* it when people don't tell me things! Why do you think that because I'm only ten I can't understand anything? Everyone always leaves me out. I *hate* it."

"Jane, please try to calm down," Mrs. Miller warned.

"Okay! Okay! Forget it! I don't even want to know." She flung herself out of the kitchen and hurtled into her bedroom. She fell on the bed and pulled the spread over her legs.

Gradually she began to feel the clammy bathing suit against her skin and she peeled it off. She stopped. Maybe

Jeff had received his military notice that day. Maybe that's why they were all so awful. It had nothing to do with her.

Yes, that must be it. Jeff would be going away to war, and they were all afraid to tell her. He could lose an arm or a leg and come home too sick to go to college. He could be killed. And he would be leaving her here alone.

She pulled on a pair of shorts and a halter. She swept the pile of wet sand under her bed and hid the bathing suit in the corner of the closet, then ran through the living room and yanked open the screen door. She dropped to her knees in front of Grandpa's chair.

"Grandpa, Grandpa . . . has Jeff been drafted? Is that what it is? Is that why you and Mother are crying? Is he leaving? *Tell me!*"

Grandpa slowly turned and gazed at Jane as if he were in a kind of trance. He looked away without speaking.

"I know something awful is happening here, Grandpa, but if someone doesn't tell me, I'm going to die. I'm going to *die*! Do you want me to die? Do you? Because I will if someone doesn't talk to me."

"Ah, Janie, it is . . . it is . . ." Grandpa's mouth was dry and his voice sounded rusty.

"Please, Grandpa, tell me and I promise I'll never ask you another thing."

"It's so terrible . . . it is so terrible, Jane, that I cannot even . . . I cannot even . . ." He covered his face with his hands, and the satin yarmulke fell to the ground. Jane brushed off the little skullcap and handed it back to him.

"Thank you," he said.

"Grandpa, I'm waiting . . . please!"

"It seems, Jane . . . it seems . . . if we are to believe it, and we think that we must believe it—"

"Believe what?"

"It appears that in Europe . . . in Germany and Poland . . . and even in France . . . there are concentration camps—"

"You mean where they are keeping Jews prisoners?"

"Yes." Grandpa looked at Jane with surprise. "How do you know that?"

"Grandpa, what do you think I am? I read it in Daddy's paper and I hear it on the radio. Didn't they take all those prisoners because they're against Hitler?"

"More because Hitler is against the Jews, Jane. And political prisoners . . . do you know about them?"

"Yes, I think so. They're really against what Hitler does, aren't they?"

"You just amaze me. Yes, they hate what he's doing to Germany and to the world. Did you hear that on the radio too?"

"And one night in temple the rabbi was talking about the Jews in the camps and the Gypsies."

"Yes," said Grandpa, sighing deeply.

"Do they mean Gypsies with tambourines and big hoop earrings and stuff like that?"

"Sometimes. Not always. They travel around and earn their living doing different things."

"Gypsies don't like to be in one place all the time?" asked Jane.

"No. It must be agonizing for them to be cooped up like that, in all that hell."

"Are the Jews in there just like us, Grandpa?"

"Yes, just like us. Even, I think . . ." And Grandpa blew his nose as a deep sob escaped from his throat.

"You think what?"

"I think we may have some relatives in the camps, particularly the ones in Poland."

"Are they going to get out now?"

"No. Oh, God, no. They are . . . they were—"

"They were *what*? Is this what everyone is crying about? *Tell* me, Grandpa."

"*Ahhhh, ahhhhh,* Janie. We have learned today that these people . . . all these people, but particularly the Jews, have been starved and beaten and . . ." Grandpa bent forward and put his hands on top of his head as if to protect himself from deadly blows.

"Do you think they were . . . killed there too?" she asked. "Were all these people killed by Hitler?"

"By the Nazis, yes. Yes, they have probably all been killed, although there may be some survivors."

"How?"

"By starvation and beatings and—I cannot tell you, Jane."

"Grandpa, you *must*, you *must*."

"Oh, God, they may have been put into showers and gassed—"

"What do you mean, *gassed* ?"

"They were evidently told that they were going to take showers and . . ." Grandpa hit his forehead as if trying to punish himself for the things he was saying.

"And they died from the gas?"

"Yes, and we think they were then . . . oh, God . . . put into ovens—"

"Ovens? No, Grandpa! What are you talking about!"

"This is what we didn't want to tell you, Jane. Don't ask me anything else."

"You mean they were put into ovens and burned up?"

"Yes, that is exactly what I mean."

"Oh, *no,* Grandpa, *no,*" cried Jane, and she reached out for her grandfather as he held his arms open to her. They clung together.

"Ah, Jane, they are burning our people, my cousins and my uncles and aunts—"

"And mine too? Are they mine too?"

Grandpa straightened up and cupped Jane's pointed chin in his hand. "They are your cousins too. And aunts and uncles and friends and rabbis and teachers and farmers—"

"Oh, Grandpa, please don't cry anymore, please don't." Jane leaned her head on his knees. "I'm so sorry about the tree . . . I'm sorry."

"I know you are."

"Do you think they will come over here and put us in the ovens too?"

"No, no, absolutely not. We are safe here," he said, smoothing back the hair from Jane's face.

"But will they bomb us the way they are bombing people over there? Like the London blitz?"

"No, no. We are too strong a country, a great, great country. But we'll never be the same. Too much has happened, and we know a lot of it now. Oh, all those little children—"

"How do you know this is all true? How did we find out?"

"A man named Jan Karski was in the camps, and he escaped and went to report all this to Winston Churchill and Anthony Eden in London—and they told President Roosevelt; and there are reports now, issued by Roosevelt and Eden . . . worse reports than you could possibly imagine."

"Worse than you have told me?"

"Yes, I fear so."

"Tell me."

"No. It's just unspeakable."

"Oh, Grandpa, are you sure that they won't come over here to get us?"

"Yes, I'm sure. But you see how careful you have to be of your heart and your soul, don't you? Do you see why sometimes it's so hard to be a Jew?"

"You mean all those people were killed just because they were Jews?"

"Yes," Grandpa barely whispered.

"But why? What did they do?"

"There are just those who hate Jews, although no one more than Hitler."

"But why?"

"I'm not sure. Maybe because we love God and not dictators. Or because we believe in books and learning. Perhaps because God made us the Chosen People . . . I don't know."

"But would all those Jews have become something else if it could have saved their lives?"

"I doubt it. Judaism is very powerful. You cannot just 'give it up.' It is what you are."

"But I am a Jew, Grandpa. I know you don't think so anymore. But I am, and I know I shouldn't have had the tree."

"No, Jane, you should not have."

"I'll never do it again. I don't even *want* another one. I promise . . . I'll never have another tree. I'll try to be a better Jew—you'll see."

"I hope so. It's up to you, such a decision. Do you understand what I'm saying? You do it because, in your heart, it's your own true choice. Because for you there is no other choice. Not because your grandfather wants it. That's what we call faith. And such faith can make you sing and dance." Grandpa looked down at Jane. His eyes were stern. "But it isn't easy. Especially in this place. All these churches . . . churches on every corner, you know."

"I want to have faith, Grandpa. I do."

"And particularly in a town called Corpus Christi it is not easy to be a Jew."

"No, Grandpa, I can do it. I know you don't think this is a good place, but I can do it here."

Jane rose and put her hands into her grandfather's. "I can't stand it when you're mad at me."

Grandpa clasped his hands together, encompassing Jane's so that they completely disappeared. "No tree, Jane, *ever*! No tree."

"Never," she swore.

"I will forgive you this time. God will forgive you. I

think. But you're the only one who can decide how you will live now. Not your mother or your father or Jeff."

"I know. I just wanted to try Christmas once—"

"*No!*" he thundered. *"Not even once."*

"I understand, Grandpa . . . I understand."

"I don't want to ever have to tear my shirt again."

"You won't. You won't. I promise," said Jane, clinging to him. "Can you put the shirt back together again?"

"Not exactly, but it will be the same as if I could," answered Grandpa, standing up and stretching.

"What do you mean?" asked Jane as she stood to join him, and a slight breeze whisked through her hair.

"God will know," he said, "if you promise never to—"

"I promised already. How many times do I have to do it?"

Grandpa raised his arms over his head. "Promise on the lives of your children."

"I don't have any children!"

"But you will. Promise on their lives, Jane."

"I promise! Now what will God know? What did you mean?"

Grandpa, lowering his arms, looked puzzled. "God will know *what*? What are you talking about?"

"About what you said!" cried Jane, beginning to run in crazy circles.

"About *what*?" asked Grandpa as he bent over to pick up his suitcase.

"About your shirt, your *shirt*! When I asked if you could mend it, you said it would be the same as—"

"As what?"

"That's what I'm asking you, Grandpa!"

"Oh, why didn't you say so? Well, let's see, it will be the same as mended . . . because God will know—"

"He will know *what*, Grandpa? *Please!*"

"He will know . . . that we've . . . that we've made up, Janie. And that you are beginning to understand about being a Jew."

All at once the rumbling of the trucks and the crackling of the announcer's voice and the children laughing on the beach became louder than before. Grandpa looked down solemnly at his high-top shoes. One lace had come undone and was dragging in the dust and sand. Jane studied her hands as if they were brand-new and then brushed an imaginary piece of lint from her sleeve. Grandpa cleared his throat. Straightening his yarmulke, he looked up at the sky as if he were sure the messiah was now going to descend, and he stood there waiting for him.

The silence—punctuated by the traffic, the surf, the radio, the children's voices—seemed to go on forever. Jane was afraid to speak for fear she would break the spell of forgiveness. What if she had just dreamed it?

"Grandpa, does God know that all those Jews have been killed?"

"I think He does, Janie."

"And the political prisoners and the Gypsies?"

"Yes, those too."

"But you always said that God is a just God."

"He is."

"Then how could He have allowed all these things to happen?"

Grandpa pulled at his vest and shifted his suitcase to

the other hand. Again he cleared his throat. His cheeks and chin began to quiver slightly, and he looked very, very old.

"I can't answer that right now," he said.

Chapter 24

Pebbles and surf-smoothed stones on the beach, the worn place in the rug near the front door, the three shades of green in the leafy pattern on Grandma's china: suddenly certain things became very clear to Jane. Had they always been there? An irregular piece of mesh in her curtains and a lightning-shaped crack in the wall stood out like miniature paintings. Some mornings she saw them, and then they disappeared again into the background.

Jane put her hairbrush on the dresser and noticed a rough gray place in the black plastic and a few bristles that splayed out from under the top of the brush. It was scary, somehow, and she quickly bent in the bristles to join the others.

Soon it would be time to go back to school. Now that the tree was gone, her blouses and shorts had been lowered once more to the bottom rung in her closet. Sometimes Jane could almost see the little tree, like a transparent pine ghost, waiting in place.

The *Corpus Christi Caller-Times* had printed a terrible picture of prisoners in a concentration camp in Vught, The Netherlands. Mr. Miller, sitting on the rickety stool in the kitchen, had wept. Mrs. Miller had put her arms around him, and it was the first time in weeks Jane could remember seeing her parents touch. Mrs. Miller seemed tender, as she was in the wedding pictures with Daddy. Daddy had looked husky and young then, his head outlined against the faces of his stocky Russian family.

Grandpa moved slowly around the house and prayed more often. The radio was still talking about the millions of people who probably had been killed. Or were still living, sick and starving, in death camps all over Europe. How long had they been there? She could not even imagine and was afraid to think about it too much.

Uncle Burt and Uncle Mel had called from Chicago, the first time since the Millers had come to Corpus Christi, and with hushed and troubled voices they had handed the phone back and forth to one another, like a baby to be coddled and treasured. Jane was amazed at her cousins' Chicago accents. She felt a jolt of homesickness.

Jeffrey had volunteered for the Army Air Force, where he was to take a test for Officers' Candidate School. He was not going to wait to be drafted; Mr. and Mrs. Miller, tense and quiet, had driven him into town. Holding his hand, Jane sat as close to Jeff as she could. What if the air force took him away tomorrow? The war was going on forever.

Lovely Jeffrey. With a thousand freckles spotting his suddenly white face, his dark red hair washed and sprouting from his head like new weeds, he had stood in front of the recruiting sergeant and offered his services to the United States of America.

"Will I get to fly an airplane?" Jeff asked.

"Yes," answered the sergeant, "if you stay in school until June and can pass the test." Jeff, looking pleased and frightened all at once, shook the sergeant's hand.

Through the walls that night, Jane heard her mother and father murmuring until the light outside went from black to pink-streaked gray.

Grandpa had made reservations for the train. This time he was going to keep them.

"Grandpa, can't you stay for a little while more?" Jane was helping Grandpa pack his suitcase. His clothes and merchandise from the sample case were spread out on the cot in Daddy's office.

"No, Janie. My customers are waiting for me, and I mustn't disappoint them."

"But you're so upset now. Why don't you wait another week?"

"Everyone is upset, dear. But life continues, and I have to leave and do my work, like everyone else."

They were sitting outside in the late afternoon, and although the sun was hot, the night before had been so chilly that all the gas heaters had been lighted. As the temperature rose and the trees began to dry and curl, she had changed into her shorts and taken off her new saddle shoes. It had been hard to take off the shoes. Daddy had finally let her buy them during the vacation, and she had joyfully thrown away her brown, ugly ones.

But now she was leaning against Grandpa's shoulder, and he had his arm around her. From the frayed cuff near her face came the familiar mixed odor of herring and starch and men's after-shave lotion. Her toes moving in the sparse grass, she said, "Will you come for Passover, Grandpa?"

"If God spares me, Jane. But you know, your uncles like to have me do the seder in Chicago."

"Maybe we could go there."

But Jane knew there was no money for the trip, and Grandpa knew it too. He looked away. "Well, Janie . . . yes, perhaps. Wouldn't that be nice?"

"Couldn't you call your customers and tell them that you'll be delayed a little?"

"No, Jane."

"But Grandpa, I worry about you. You're sad now. Everyone is so sad. How will you feel like selling anything at all?"

"God will give me the strength . . . and the will."

"How?"

"He will protect me."

"Oh, Grandpa, you always say that. *How* will He protect you?"

"He'll take care of me the way He sheltered the rabbi from the raindrops."

"What rabbi?" Here comes another of Grandpa's stories, she thought. She smiled. She was sure he made up most of them anyway.

"Oh, once there was a young rabbi . . . he had very

little experience. He lived in Poland, and the winter was cold and merciless. But in the next town was going to take place an exceptionally holy wedding . . . of a beloved Yeshiva student and a beautiful girl."

"And I'll bet the girl had a rich father," added Jane.

Grandpa laughed. "Yes, I imagine she did, but that's not what matters."

"What matters?" asked Jane, nestling her head against his arm.

"Well, the day before the wedding the young rabbi's coat was stolen, and he couldn't afford to buy another one, and his shoes were full of holes. In those days, you know, people didn't have galoshes and umbrellas and raincoats in the *shtetls* of Poland."

"I know. So did the rich girl's father send him a horse and buggy?"

"No. Who's telling this story?"

"Me," said Jane.

"No. I am," replied Grandpa, kissing Jane's hair.

"Okay, you are."

"So, now, let me see . . . where was I?"

"The rabbi had no coat."

"Ah, yes. The rabbi had no coat. So he went to *shul* and made a little prayer to God. 'God,' he said, 'I have to marry these two wonderful people, but if I go in this weather, I may get sick and not be able to come back and lead my congregation. What should I do?' "

" 'Well,' God said, 'Rabbi, you must trust me. Go to the town and make the wedding. I will take care of you.' "

" 'But God,' argued the rabbi, 'it might rain tomorrow. What if I get all wet?' "

"Grandpa, this rabbi is a dodo bird."

"No, Janie . . . I told you, he was just inexperienced."

"But he seems to be afraid of everything."

"Sometimes we're afraid until we learn to trust God."

"So did the rabbi go?"

"Yes, he did. The next day the rain came down in great sheets, and the rabbi said to God, 'God, are you really going to protect me?'

" 'I am,' He said, 'Just go out there and walk between the raindrops.'

" 'Walk between the raindrops? Excuse me, God, but that is not possible.'

" 'Oh, yes,' God said, 'not one inch of your suit will be wet. But you must believe in Me.'

"So the rabbi put his prayerbook and *tallis* and a clean shirt into an old cloth bag and started out."

"And did he get wet?"

"No. Not a drop. When he got to the house of the bride, everyone was astonished that he was completely dry. 'How did this happen?' they cried.

" 'I walked between the raindrops,' he announced. 'God guided me along the way.' The people touched him and turned him around and around and considered it an absolute miracle."

"Oh, Grandpa, how could anyone do that—walk between raindrops?"

"It's a story of faith, Janie. If you cherish being a Jew and follow your religion—"

"And trust in God—"

"Yes, Jane . . . trust in God . . . the way will be shown."

"If we trust in God now, do you think we'll understand about the concentration camps and Hitler and all the Jews someday?"

"Oh, little girl, I hope so." Grandpa's face seemed to dissolve for a moment, and Jane was sorry she had asked. She stroked his arm and said quickly, "But Grandpa, how did he *actually* walk that way?"

"Oh, I can show you," he said, rising slowly. Jane held his elbow until he was steady. "Now, you watch me and I'll demonstrate." Grandpa mopped his eyes and stuffed his handkerchief into his back pocket.

Holding his arms high, he began to walk toward the highway, his hips and storklike legs swinging from side to side like a Spanish dancer's. The gravel made puffs of dust as he moved. He anchored his yarmulke with one hand, while the other kept moving in rhythm. And Jane could almost see the raindrops as he began to hum a melody: "*Ya-ya-ya-ya-ya . . .*"

"Wait for me, Grandpa. I'll come with you."

"Hurry up then. I'm almost at the wedding."

He was fast and graceful, but after a minute or so she was flying behind him—her arms, too, cutting through the air—and singing the funny little song: "*Ya-ya-ya-ya-ya . . .*"

Her tan legs shone in the sun as Jane wiggle-waggled toward the road. Mr. Garland was easing the big Cadillac out of his driveway as Jane drew parallel to Sally's house, and from a navy jeep came the voice of Burl Ives spreading out over the salty air:

Wish I had a sweetheart
I'd set her on a shelf,
And every time she smiled at me,
I'd get up there myself.
Fare thee well, Old Joe Clark
Fare thee well, I say,
He'll foller me ten thousand mile
To hear my fiddle play.

The guitar music seemed to touch her heels and lift her up from the earth. The farther away they moved from the water, the hotter it became. A gardenia bush loomed white, its fragrance so dense that she gasped. Jane sang and shook her hands like tambourines. She felt transparent, as if she and dancing, singing Grandpa were blending into the shimmering air.

Ahead she saw streaks of cars whizzing past like colored firecrackers. Where were they going? To San Antonio, Houston, Dallas, New York, the whole world. Places where orchestras played great music and there were paintings Jane had never seen. And ocean liners and ferry boats, the Atlantic Ocean and houses with open windows and shining wooden floors.

But first she would go to the university in Austin. She would work and pay her own way, no matter what, just like Jeff. She would change her life and live in a new place and move into the light. And laugh and laugh.

The cars, fired by bands of heat, seemed like beacons heading into the future. They moved away from Jane on their journeys. Someday she would go where they were going.

BARBARA BARRIE, the actress, has appeared in numerous plays, films, and television shows. She has received Drama Desk and Obie awards and was nominated for an Oscar for her role as the mother in *Breaking Away* and a Tony Award for her work in the musical *Company.* She won Best Actress at the Cannes Film Festival for the groundbreaking film *One Potato, Two Potato.* For many years she played Mrs. Miller on the television series *Barney Miller.*

Barbara Barrie was graduated from the University of Texas with a BFA in Drama. She lives in New York City with her husband, Jay Harnick, a producer and director, and their children, Jane and Aaron.

Lone Star is her first novel, and was inspired by her screenplay for *The Chanukah Bush.*